Am
GW01019273

Quest

"Can I ask you a favour?" said Ruth. "Will you be totally honest with me this trip?"

"How do you mean?"

"I mean – if you get us lost, will you say so at once and not bluff."

"I've got us lost," I said.

"Thank you," said Ruth. "You may find it hard to believe, but that makes me feel better."

"I know exactly where we're trying to go," I said, defensively. "I just don't know exactly where we are."

"I'll tell you where we are," said Ruth. "We're standing outside a great-looking café. Why are we outside when we could be inside?"

It's true that I was the one who sent the case off into oblivion on the conveyor belt. However, Ruth was the one who chose the café run by the Paranoid-Depressive.

Judy Allen has written over 30 published titles. She has won the Earthworm Award, the Whitbread Children's Novel Award and been Commended for the Carnegie Medal.

Amsterdam
Quest

Judy Allen

RED FOX

A Red Fox Book

Published by Random House Children's Books
20 Vauxhall Bridge Road, London SW1V 2SA

A division of Random House UK Ltd
London Melbourne Sydney Auckland
Johannesburg and agencies throughout the world

1 3 5 7 9 10 8 6 4 2

First published simultaneously in hardback and paperback by
Julia MacRae and Red Fox 1996

Phototypeset by Intype, London
Printed and bound in Great Britain by
Cox & Wyman Ltd, Reading, Berkshire

RANDOM HOUSE UK Limited Reg. No. 954009

Papers used by Random House UK Limited
are natural, recyclable products made from wood
grown in sustainable forests. The manufacturing
processes conform to the environmental regulations
of the country of origin.

ISBN 0 09 943711 2

For Nicola

CONTENTS

CHAPTER ONE

The Wow Cake

I was certain I knew what would happen when I told Ruth the good news. It was nearly two hours before I found out I was wrong.

I wanted to leave work early to tell her at once, but we were too busy. I couldn't even use the phone. Most of the time the lines were blocked with people booking hotels, or fixing flights, or checking up on package holidays. The rest of the time they were blocked by people asking stupid questions – ("No, Madam, I can't guarantee that your plane won't be hijacked, but statistically it's extremely unlikely".)

The moment Peggy turned the sign on the door around so it said Closed, I took off at speed for Ruth's house.

Ruth's younger brother, George, opened the door. "Yo, Jo!" he said, punching the air. He's half-English and he's lived over here most of his life, but sometimes he sounds more American than Ruth. "Come in," he said, "Ruth's in the kitchen, making me an egg omelette."

I followed him through to where Ruth stood with

her back to me, stirring something beside the cooker. "With you in a second," she said.

She didn't seem about to turn round so I leant on the door and began to talk to the back of her head. Ruth has a lot of red hair, with silver and turquoise beads threaded on the bit that grows down the middle. It has such a strong character, Ruth's hair, that I almost felt I could tell it the story and it would relay it to Ruth through her scalp.

"Listen carefully!" I said. "Because this is unbelievable . . ." But before I could say any more, Ruth interrupted.

"It has to be!" she said. "Today is National Unbelievable day. Do you realise how hard I struggled to pass exams just to end up cooking for a small ungrateful male who's perfectly capable of getting his own food?"

"You're not doing it because you're the girl," said George. "You're doing it because you're the grown-up. Also you make great egg omelettes."

"Why is it," said Ruth, beating the mixture wildly and splashing tiny yellow drops onto the wall, "that it drives me crazy when he calls them egg omelettes?"

"I don't know," I said politely. I tried to work out what she was really upset about. I failed.

"It shouldn't matter," Ruth went on, "but for some reason it *does*. George – *all* omelettes are made with egg. You can have cheese omelettes, tomato omelettes, anything omelettes. *Or* you can have a plain omelette – like this," she tipped the mixture into the pan, "which is what you said you wanted. There is no such expression as 'egg omelette'. Okay?"

The Wow Cake

"Okay," said George. He sat down at the table and looked up at me. "She's really cranky today," he said.

"I've a right to be," said Ruth. "I'm sorry, Jo, I'll get this out of my system soon, it's just that I'm wasting my year off. Next fall I'll be at college. This year was supposed to be for high earning, high spending and high adventure. But the only job I can find is looking out for my kid brother in return for small change. I even flunked minding the twins next door."

"You didn't," I said, because it was true. "It was just that their grandmother went into a decline when she was deprived of them."

It's very hard to stay in announcement-mode when no one's really listening. I sagged against the door and tried to rev up my enthusiasm again.

I'd had a problem finding work too. I'd ended up as temporary office junior in Quest Travel, which is the travel agency my father runs. At the same time, I'm temporary office junior in Quest Tours, which is the company my mother runs in the offices above Quest Travel. You might wonder why I don't give one of my jobs to Ruth. There is a reason. I may have two jobs, but I only have one salary – and it's small.

Ruth flicked the omelette over neatly and slid it onto George's plate. He settled himself comfortably on his chair and seized his knife and fork. "Egg omelettes are my favourite," he said.

"Ruth," I said quickly, determined to get her attention before she exploded again. "Listen, will you. We've had a call from Philippe's father."

Philippe's father is a tour operator in Paris. Philippe's parents and mine know each other through

3

work, and Ruth and I met Philippe last year when he came over on a six week student exchange. As Ruth put it at the time, he definitely has a high cuteness factor.

"Go on," said Ruth, perking up. She leant across the cooker to mop the egg off the wall with a dishcloth.

"Dad told them the whole story," I said, "about our . . . our . . ."

"Adventure!" said George with his mouth full. "Ruth said it was an adventure."

"Right, our adventure, and they were as impressed with us as Dad was . . . listen to this, Ruth . . . now we get to the good bit . . ."

"I need a good bit!" said Ruth, turning to face me at last. "Hurry up!"

"I am," said George, scraping his fork against his plate with a horrible screeching sound.

"Not you, her," said Ruth.

"They want us to visit them," I said. I was beginning to jig about where I stood. "They want to show us around . . . take us out to eat . . ."

"To eat . . ." said Ruth dreamily.

"Well, they can't believe we went to Paris and didn't sample French cuisine. They've fixed our flights and Dad's giving us some spending money."

"Why?" said Ruth. "Why would they do that?"

"Because when Philippe was over last year everyone treated him to stuff, but we never did the other half of the exchange so they think they owe us . . . and they're sorry they missed us in Paris last week . . . and they've had a cancellation. Dad's forking out because he says we deserve a reward. You just have to get your parents to say yes, but there isn't much time. It's all set up – it's take it or leave it – and I don't want to leave it!"

I knew exactly what would happen next. Ruth would fling the dishcloth in the air and start to laugh. Then we'd begin to talk about what clothes to pack. Later we'd discuss whether we'd prefer a boat trip on the Seine or a guided tour through the Paris sewers – that kind of thing.

I was wrong, though. It didn't happen like that. Ruth just stood there. Then she said, "You mean they went ahead and fixed it? Without checking with us? We might have had dates or something!"

"You've *been* to Paris," said George. "Why isn't it my turn?"

"Because no one's going to let you take time off school," said Ruth. She dumped the cloth and rolled an apple towards him along the kitchen table. "Eat that and let me get my head around this."

"You didn't even bring me a present," said George. He sounded quite resigned about it, but Ruth came over all guilty at once.

"Oh George," she said, "I keep telling you I'm sorry about that. I didn't forget, we just didn't have time to look for anything."

"You had time to meet all those men you kept talking about," said George. "And I *am* your best brother."

"You're my only brother."

"I must be the best, then," said George. "When are you going?"

"Day after tomorrow," I said. "I suppose it was a bit pushy of them. I was too excited to notice."

"You'll miss Mum's birthday," said George.

"Hell fire," said Ruth. "And George is unhappy already and I don't know what Gareth's going to think about it . . ."

I looked at her in amazement. This was not the Ruth I thought I knew – confident, positive, enthusiastic. It completely threw me to see her standing in the middle of the kitchen, twisting her silver rings and looking anxious.

"What's the matter with you?" I said. "George is fine – aren't you, George? And we can bring your mother back a special present – *and* one for you, George – *and* one for Gareth if you like. This will be a normal trip – this will be a trip where we get to go shopping."

"Mum'll be okay about it," said George, through a mouthful of apple. "She'll have Dad and me. It'll cost you a WOW cake, though."

"I'd have made a WOW cake anyway," said Ruth.

I asked what a Wow cake was, but I might as well not have bothered because neither of them took any notice. "Ruth!" I said. "This is *good* news!"

"I guess I have to start branching out some time," said Ruth, thoughtfully. "It's not as if I do it often."

"It's not as if you're a problem teenager," I said.

"It's not as if you're a young offender!" said George.

"Please!" said Ruth. "I'm a model daughter."

"Not even a rebel," I said.

"How can I be," said Ruth, "with parents like mine?"

I knew what she meant. Ruth's mother manages a small DIY shop and doesn't buy rainforest timber and tries to talk people out of using toxic chemicals on their woodwork. Her father works for an environmental organisation in New York. Her step-father, George's Dad, teaches environmental studies in London. Difficult to argue with any of that. Must be annoying, sometimes.

"I have an idea," said Ruth. "We'll go to the supermarket right now and get the stuff for the cake . . ."

"What *is* this cake?" I said.

". . . then I can see Gareth. He's working every night this week – I don't want to call him about this, I want to talk to him properly."

I've always known there are two main types of boy-friend trouble. One is not having a boy-friend. The other is having a boy-friend. I don't usually make this public, but I have the first problem. I've always thought it would be much nicer to have the second problem. Looking at Ruth now, though, I wasn't quite so sure.

"Gareth won't mind, will he?" I said.

"Think about it!" said Ruth. "There he is, spending his year off shelf-stacking, and here am I, planning to fly the Channel twice in ten days! Plus I'm probably going to spend the Christmas holiday in New York with my father."

"But I can't imagine Gareth being difficult about it," I said.

"He acted strange about the last trip," said Ruth.

I realised I didn't know Gareth as well as Ruth did, but that really surprised me. "He always seems so laid back," I said.

"We'll see," said Ruth. "George, you'll have to

come too – I can't leave you – Dad won't be back for an hour."

"Okay," said George, who likes Gareth.

A nasty thought came to me. "But you will come?" I said. "Whatever Gareth says, you will come? If you can't rebel against your parents at least you can rebel against your boy-friend!"

"She has already," said George. "They had a fight on the phone yesterday."

"We did not!" said Ruth. "Come on, let's go."

"*You have to tell me what a wow cake is!*" I said, to give myself time to adjust to the new – but definitely not improved – Ruth.

"Last year I made a cake for Mothering Sunday and wrote MOM on the top in icing," said Ruth. "George read it upside down – and we decided his version was an improvement."

"What do we buy to make it with?" I said, expecting some exotic ingredients.

"Chocolate," said George.

"I think I might have to get some boring stuff to hold the chocolate together," said Ruth. "Like flour and eggs . . ."

"There's flour in the cupboard," said George.

"You must have at least one brain cell," said Ruth, "or you wouldn't be alive. I can't make a WOW cake with the WOW's own ingredients!"

"Ruth," I said, deciding to catch her while she sounded a bit bouncier. "You *will* come to France with me?"

"I guess so," said Ruth. "Maybe."

Up till that moment, despite the fact that Ruth was being so sludgy about everything, it hadn't really

occurred to me that we might not be going together.
Now it did occur to me. I didn't like it at all.

You might think I'd be glad to have the cute
Philippe to myself. You'd be wrong. Philippe is quite
sophisticated. Ruth and I together can have a good
laugh with him. When I'm alone with him, I get
embarrassed and can't think of anything to say. It
just wouldn't be any fun without Ruth.

I know you're not supposed to interfere in other
people's relationships. Even so, I planned to take
Gareth aside and say something very fierce to him.

CHAPTER TWO

Under Suspicion

All the way to the supermarket I was trying to decide how to open my attack on Gareth. Should I go straight for it? Should I say, 'Does it really make you feel good to spoil Ruth's chance of a holiday, you creep?' Or was that a little bit strong?

Might it be better to give him a subtle advance warning that he was in trouble. Should I open with 'I've got a bone to pick with you'? I've heard people use that quite effectively. It's an odd expression, though, and it gets odder the longer you think about it. It begins to sound quite festive. In fact it begins to sound like an invitation to a barbecue.

As soon as we actually saw Gareth, though, all my ferocious intentions faded. He simply doesn't look like a bad guy. He's stocky, chunky, reliable-looking, somehow. He has a smiley face, curly hair and seven small silver rings in one ear. He just didn't arouse my killer-instincts.

We found him in Wines and Spirits, standing inside a protective circle of 'Danger Wet Floor' cones. He was sweeping up an enormous red puddle with lumps of green broken glass in it. For one nightmare moment I thought the red stuff was blood. (Judging by George's initial excitement, so did he.) But Gareth said it was only Chianti.

"Good grief," said Ruth, "someone must have dropped it from a great height."

"She was a tall woman," nodded Gareth, leaning on the broom. "An interesting case. I could see she couldn't make up her mind whether to buy it or not. So she dropped it to get out of having to make the decision."

"You mean she dropped it on purpose?" said George. "Did she get into trouble?"

"Couldn't it have been a genuine accident?" said Ruth.

"It's not as simple as that," said Gareth. "It *was* a genuine accident, yes. On the other hand, there *are* no accidents."

"Gareth," I said, "you make things very complicated."

"Things already are complicated," said Gareth cheerfully. "It's just that I'm aware of it. If you want to study human behaviour, this is your place."

Almost as if to prove him right, an elderly man in a black tracksuit and black woolly hat came up beside him and tapped him on the shoulder. "Now then, young man," he said, "have you checked for me today?"

"I have," said Gareth. "I had a look in the stock-room an hour ago and they're stacked up to the ceiling."

"You're a good lad," said the man as he pottered off.

"No worries," said Gareth.

11

"What's stacked to the ceiling?" said Ruth.

"Kitchen foil," said Gareth. "He says the geomagnetic storms in the upper atmosphere give him headaches unless he blocks the rays by wearing kitchen foil under his clothes. He buys a roll a day and he likes to be sure we're not going to run out."

George stared after him. "He doesn't *look* mad," he said. "Not really."

"Who says he is?" said Gareth. "Science may prove him right one day. You want madness? We stock a cosmetic that says it can make a 40-year-old look like a 20-year-old – and people *buy* it. Is that weird or is that weird?"

"I thought advertising wasn't allowed to lie," said Ruth.

"I expect there's a loophole," said Gareth. "To be fair, it just says 'Over 40? Would you like the skin of a 20-year-old?' – it doesn't say a 20-year-old what."

"This cream," I said, striking a pose, "is guaranteed to make you look like a 20-year-old warthog."

"Unfortunately," said Gareth, copying my pose, "warthogs only live for 10 years."

"Do they?" said George. "They always look really old, don't they, warthogs?"

"You're missing the point, George," said Ruth. "Go find some flour."

"Yes," I said firmly, "enough of this chat." I shunted George ahead of me, off into the depths of the store.

By the time Ruth caught up with us we were three stacks away, level with the shampoos and moving fast.

"George can manage," hissed Ruth, grabbing me

by the arm and almost colliding with a case of lipsticks opposite. "You don't have to go with him."

George, completely unaware that I'd stopped, stomped on ahead, swinging the basket. As I opened my mouth to call him he reached the conditioners, turned right, and vanished.

I began to explain to Ruth that I'd walked away to be tactful. At the same time Ruth began to explain to me that she'd wanted me to stick around and give my opinion of Gareth's reaction. It was while we were trying to shout each other down in whispers (in case Gareth was in hearing range) that I noticed we were under surveillance.

"That security man doesn't like the look of us," I said.

"Then he has no taste," said Ruth, glancing over her shoulder.

"Don't look round like that," I said, "it makes you look furtive."

I realised I was glancing round just as furtively myself.

The security guard began to stroll down the aisle towards us, very, very casually but very, very purposefully.

"Come on," said Ruth, completely ignoring the ominous approach. "Let's get this Gareth conversation over with. He's not exactly supposed to entertain visitors at work. I don't want to get him into trouble."

"If we move now," I hissed, "just as Action Man's closing in, we'll *really* look like criminals."

"But we're not doing anything wrong," said Ruth, walking off.

She was right, of course, but then so was I.

"See," I hissed at her, "he's following us."

"If he is," said Ruth, "it's only because you're looking so guilty."

"We are textbook shoplifters," I said. "Hanging around the cosmetics, whispering. *And* we haven't even got a basket."

"George has our basket."

"How does that help?"

"Cool it! He's not the Secret Police. What can he do?"

"Stop and search?" I said.

"What a revolting thought," said Ruth, looking briefly over her shoulder again. "You have a sick mind. Keep walking."

He tracked us all the way back to Gareth. Then he paused, a short distance off, and just watched.

"Is that security guard senior to you or junior?" said Ruth.

"I don't worry about hierarchy," said Gareth. "Everyone's here to do his or her own job, that's all."

"Okay, so he's senior," said Ruth. "We'd better move on. Don't want to make him suspicious of you, too."

I couldn't bear to think of Ruth avoiding the essential conversation yet again.

"Tell him we're okay," I said to Gareth. "Tell him he could be missing out on all kinds of evil-doing while he's wasting time shadowing us."

"No worries," said Gareth, "he's gone now. Anyway, it's not a good idea to talk to the security guards when they're on duty. They don't like to have attention drawn to them. They need to be discreet."

"*Discreet?*" said Ruth. "This guy is wearing a uniform and openly following people. We're not dealing with an undercover operation here."

"You're getting side-tracked *yet* again," I said.

And then I understood – at last. Ruth wanted me to make the announcement about the trip. She wasn't actually going to ask me to do it, nothing so simple. She was just going to faff about until I couldn't stand the suspense any more and got on with it.

I braced myself for an abrupt change of mood from Gareth. Then I went right to it.

"Ruth and I've been invited to stay with some friends of my parents in Paris," I said, straightening my shoulders and gritting my teeth ready for the argument.

"Great!" said Gareth. "Are you using the tunnel?"

"No, they've got some special airline deal."

"Shame," said Gareth. "When do you go?"

"In a couple of days," I said, relaxing my shoulders a bit. "Just for a long weekend."

"Terrific," said Gareth. "Your last visit was too short. An insult to a beautiful city."

"You don't mind?" said Ruth.

"Why would I?" said Gareth. "Are you going to ask to borrow money, or something?"

At that point a store supervisor, in a suit and name badge, appeared from behind the beer fridges and began to move in our direction.

For a moment I thought the security guard – who had reappeared down the other end of the aisle – must have sent for him. Then I saw his clipboard and realised he was simply planning to check the Australian wines. Even so, it seemed unlikely that he'd be impressed to find Gareth the centre of a small social gathering.

"We'd better move on," I said.

"It might be a good idea," said Gareth, who had cleared up the mess and gathered up the cones. "I'm supposed to take these to Baby Foods. There's been an incident with some pureed banana."

So the three of us left Gareth and went in search of George. Ruth and I walked ahead. The security guard padded grimly along behind.

"Do you suppose people'll think he's our chauffeur?" I said.

"No," said Ruth.

We found George hanging around near one of the check-outs. He was so angry he looked as though he might spontaneously combust. He had all the right stuff in his wire basket – flour, chocolate, eggs, icing sugar – and he was outraged that he'd been left to collect it by himself.

"That was a mean trick," he said. "And you needn't think I'm going to pay for it because I haven't got any money. You *know* I haven't got any money. Did you expect me to steal it, or what?"

The security guard closed in . . . "Are you all together?" he asked.

"Yes," I began nervously, wondering how a criminal record would affect my career curve, "but . . ."

"Oh, hi!" said George. Then he turned and glared at Ruth again. "He helped me find the icing sugar," he said, "when you *abandoned* me."

The security guard listened impassively while we explained ourselves to George. Then he patted

George on the head and said, "The lad's a bit young to do the errands while you gossip, you know."

Normally, George hates being patronised by adults. Normally, he would have snarled out something about being perfectly capable. This time, though, he looked smugly at us and said, with a slight quaver in his voice, "It's okay. I managed."

The security guard gave him a compassionate smile, glanced at us with deep distaste, and loped off on his beat.

"I don't even believe this," said Ruth, when she'd paid for the shopping and we'd all bundled out into the street. "My brother is a creep. And Gareth is still being weird."

I said I'd never seen anybody be less weird than Gareth.

Ruth made a face. "He was just as weird as he was when I told him about the first trip," she said.

"He thought it was a great idea!" I said.

"That's what I *mean*," said Ruth. "He doesn't mind."

Not for the first time, I realised things were more complicated than I'd thought. "You mean you *want* him to mind?"

"Of course I do. He ought to be jealous. I think he's losing interest, Jo. Maybe he's already lost it."

"Rubbish – he's behaving like a normal, reasonable person."

"I wonder if it's because I'm taller than him . . ."

"I can't stand it when you get like this," I said. "I remember now – you did it once before, when the twins' grandmother was so helpful. You decided that was because you were a failure, too."

17

"Did you notice he didn't kiss me when we met?" said Ruth.

"Aaaaaah," said George, whose anger had completely evaporated. He began to kiss the back of his hand with wet, slurping noises.

"Be reasonable," I said, "we were in the middle of a supermarket – he was trying to clear up a wine lake."

"He's not like he used to be," grumbled Ruth.

"You once told me," I said, getting more irritable by the minute, "that Gareth was fine for everyday but not for excitement. Doesn't sound to me as if *you're* too passionate about *him*, if you want to know."

"It's one thing for me to be unenthusiastic about him. It's not the same if he's unenthusiastic about me."

I stopped walking and stood still. Eventually Ruth noticed and came back.

George, oblivious, wandered on alone.

"What?" said Ruth.

"You've spoilt it all," I said. "I don't want you to come at all if you're going to be like this."

Ruth stared at me for a second. Then she said, "I'm sorry. You're right. But you know me, you know I can only think about one thing at a time. Okay, I've thought about Gareth. Now I'll think about the invitation." She paused briefly, then flung her arms in the air and yelled, "YIPPEEEEEEEE!"

George stopped, spun round, and ran back.

"You *left* me again . . ." he began.

"No," said Ruth, "you left us. And I called you back, didn't I?"

"Oh," said George. "I didn't know that's what you were doing. Okay."

"Forgiven?" said Ruth to me.

"Yup," I said, and I felt a grin spreading across my face.

It was all right. I stopped feeling irritated with Ruth and began to feel excited instead.

Of course – at that stage – I still believed we were going to fly to Paris in a couple of days' time and meet up with Philippe.

CHAPTER THREE

Mistaken Identity

I've always wanted to be paged at an airport, but when it happened I didn't like it at all. I had assumed it would make me feel important. In fact it made me nervous.

Ruth and I had done really well. We'd got ourselves into the terminal building more than an hour and a half before our flight, as instructed by the airline. This was good going, considering our flight was a hideously early one.

We'd decided not to go straight into the departure lounge, on the grounds that there were fewer ways of killing time in there. However, we had checked our single bulging piece of luggage through.

The original plan had been to travel light, with just one piece of hand baggage each. That plan stood no chance. Then we hit on the idea of putting everything into my huge, canvas holdall. It has a handle at each end, as well as the one in the middle, which meant we could share the weight as well as the space.

Once the bag was on its way we wandered about – spinning a few paperback stands – looking at the racks of t-shirts – trying not to spend too much money in the Body Shop – until I called a halt.

"We have to get into sophisticated, cosmopolitan mode," I said, "ready for Philippe."

"Fine," said Ruth, paying for a fruit-scented deodorant. "Any suggestions?"

"Sophisticated travellers do not walk around airport shops looking interested," I said. "They sit somewhere, looking bored. Unless they're working on their lap-top computers."

"I don't have a computer right here," said Ruth, "but I'm happy to sit and look bored, if that's what you want."

"Let's get some coffee."

"Careful," said Ruth, "you might enjoy it."

It was while we were looking around for the cafeteria that we suddenly realised what the disembodied voice echoing around the airport was actually saying. It was calling my name and telling me to go to the Information Desk.

"It's okay," said Ruth, as we struggled through crowds of sleepy-looking travellers, "it's your mother, I can see her."

I tried not to panic, but I couldn't imagine what my mother could possibly be doing here. She'd still been in bed when I left. She wasn't due in the Quest Tours office for at least two hours. I couldn't think of anything that would bring her to the airport this early – apart from bad news.

It was true that she looked perfectly calm, but then she would. She's not the sort to panic, ever. As soon as she saw us she came to meet us, then guided us to the café. When we got to the table we found it

21

had a tray of coffee and cakes already on it. She'd bought the coffee and then saved the table by leaning the chairs forward against it. If anyone else had done that, someone would have been bound to tip the chairs back, sit down, and drink the coffee. Somehow, because my mother had done it, it worked. I don't seem to have inherited her power over the universe – but I'm working on it.

"Don't look so worried," she said, "relax, have a cake. I've just come to ask you both a favour, that's all."

"Sure," said Ruth, taking a Danish pastry, "whatever."

Ruth doesn't know my mother all that well.

"It must be a big favour," I said suspiciously, "to bring you all the way out here."

"Not really," said my mother casually. "It's just that I'd like you to go to Amsterdam instead of Paris."

Ruth choked, violently.

I said, "We can't! Philippe's family are expecting us."

"They'll understand," said my mother, handing Ruth a hanky to mop her streaming eyes. "This is professional."

That got our attention. It was only a few days since we'd done our bit for my father's company, Quest Travel. It now looked as if Mum considered us suitable material to trouble-shoot for her company, Quest Tours.

"This sounds like a good career move," I said. "Am I right?"

"It could be," said my mother. "We have a family party of Americans on a Quest for Antiques Tour.

22

They're due to arrive in Amsterdam this morning to visit some specialist galleries. The problem is, the Dutch courier has called in sick. We could get a stand-in, who might be absolutely terrific for all I know – but that's the problem, I *don't* know. I don't know anything about her and these clients are important."

"Rich, huh?" said Ruth.

"Very," said my mother. "What's more, they have rich friends. If this tour goes well they could give us a lot of business. Normally, I'd have had to risk using someone I don't know – but as you two are on the move already, I'd like to divert you to handle it."

"What would we have to do?"

"Everything's been set up for weeks – a car will fetch them from the airport and take them to their hotel. All you have to do is meet them there, mid-morning, take them to a couple of galleries – where they are expected – see that they get lunch – and then shunt them around a few more galleries in the afternoon. We haven't set up appointments in the afternoon galleries, but make sure they're served by the top potato, not some junior."

"Then we go on to Paris?"

"You'll have to stay in Amsterdam overnight. Next morning is 'at leisure', but you have to be there, in case you're needed. A car will pick them up at lunch-time on the second day to take them to the airport. They fly on to Munich, where our German courier will take over. There's nothing to it – they don't actually even need a courier, but they think they do. They like to be fussed over by someone who can be polite and give the impression of being competent."

I was rather offended to realise that we hadn't been chosen for our unique and special skills. "If it's as simple as that," I said, "why not use the Dutch understudy?"

"Quest Tours has never worked with anyone I haven't personally recruited," said my mother primly, "and I don't want to start now. So – are you both saying yes?"

"I guess so," said Ruth, looking dazed.

My mother opened her briefcase and put a pile of papers and brochures on the table. "On the second day," she said, seeming not to notice that I hadn't answered, "you'll be free in time to catch the afternoon train through to Paris – here's the timetable. It's a nice journey – and it gets you into Paris Nord at about ten. Philippe says he'll meet you."

"You've called Philippe already?"

"Of course. I don't want to ruin your holiday!" She opened a guidebook, spread out the street map of Amsterdam, and began to mark things in blue ballpoint. "This is their hotel," she said, circling it, "and here are the two main galleries . . ." She drew neat, numbered arrows.

"It isn't as simple as that," I said, looking wildly round the crowded airport and wondering where to start. "How do we change the flight?"

"I've changed it," said my mother.

"We've already checked our case onto the Paris flight!"

"I do have contacts you know," said my mother. "It's loading onto the Amsterdam flight even as we speak."

"You might have asked us before you did all this!" I said. "You just assumed we'd agree!"

"There wasn't time," said my mother. "I had to get the practicalities sorted out fast. It's a shame I couldn't send the case through to Paris on its own – but security won't go for that one. But you'll be able to dump it in Left Luggage at Amsterdam Central Station before you meet your group."

Your group – she'd said 'your group'. It may have been a deliberate psychological ploy, but it worked. I began to feel enthusiastic about this. Ruth spotted it.

"Oh-oh," she said, "you're off on another power kick, I can tell." She turned to my mother. "Did you know your daughter just loves telling rich people what to do and where to go?" she said.

"That's because she's my daughter," said my mother, grinning. Then she began to hand things over to me – timetables, marked-up city map, Dutch dosh, names, brochure for the Quest for Antiques Tour, the lot. "I haven't had a chance to book you into a hotel yet," she said. "I'll do it later this morning. Call me when you arrive and I'll tell you where you're staying."

"It's all right," I said, feeling it was time I showed some initiative. "We're stand-in couriers, not clients. We'll find somewhere for ourselves."

"The company can't pay for five-star accommodation," said my mother.

"No worries," I said, picking up Gareth's phrase. "We'll find somewhere modest. Leave it to me."

"You should be on the move," said my mother, still calm. "The Amsterdam flight's boarding now,

25

and you need to pick up your new tickets at the airline desk."

Which was how we came to be sitting on the 'wrong' plane, flying to the 'wrong' city, before we had really had time to get our heads round the new arrangements.

"I don't understand how this happened," said Ruth, accepting a plastic tray of breakfast from a passing stewardess. "How come your mother found out the Amsterdam courier was sick before she even got into her office?"

"We've got a business phone and fax at home," I said. "Quest Tours and Travel never rest, you know!"

"She's very impressive in action," said Ruth.

"It's her job," I said, surprised at how proud I felt.

"She's taken care of everything," said Ruth, shaking her head in wonder. "She'd even have done the hotel if you'd let her."

"I can handle that."

"Okay," said Ruth. "So all we have to do is learn their names and get familiar with this street map. Nothing left to chance."

"Once chance knows it's dealing with my mother," I said, "it doesn't dare to mess about."

But of course the moment we left the ground, chance wasn't dealing with my mother any more, it was dealing with me. I should have remembered that chance doesn't show quite the same respect when I'm in charge.

CHAPTER FOUR

Warning in a Brown Café

Everything went perfectly until we were standing in a jam of passengers at the carousel at Schipol Airport, waiting for our bag to come off the plane.

"Look at this!" said Ruth, as a familiar green hold-all came pushing out through the flaps. "First off. Terrific!"

"That'll be because it was last on," I said, reaching out to grab it as it wobbled past us on the conveyor belt. Then I saw the label and let it go on by, feeling a sharp pang of disappointment. It wasn't ours. Someone called Mrs M. Oyting had the cheek to be travelling with an identical one.

"I thought it looked better packed than ours," said Ruth, "less lumpy."

We should have guessed then what was likely to happen. But we were talking and laughing, and trying to keep our feet as passengers pushed past us to reach out for their luggage, and then bumped into us again as they pulled it clear.

When did we realise? I'll tell you when we realised. When we were the only two passengers left beside the carousel, and the green holdall that was not ours was the only bag left, revolving mournfully all by itself. Ruth let out a desperate cry, then reached out and grabbed it as it began to pass for the umpteenth time. "I didn't mind getting the wrong airplane to the wrong city," she said. "But I do mind having the wrong bag. And whoever has all my best clothes is probably miles away by now!"

For one milli-second I thought the missing case must have flown to France by itself after all. Then I dismissed the idea. My mother is more efficient than that. Also, there was only one logical explanation for the fact that the last unclaimed piece of baggage was identical to ours.

"Quick!" I said. I grabbed a handle so that Ruth and I were carrying the thing between us. "We have to get this to the airline desk and ask them to page the owners. They may still be in the airport with our stuff."

The paging produced no result.

The airline rep was reassuring. She pointed out that there had been a genuine mistake, not a theft. We were certain to be reunited with our property. It was possible, she said, that Mrs Oyting would realise what had happened at any moment, and hurry back to the airport. Failing that, the airline would contact her as soon as she reached her destination and make arrangements to swap the bags.

"We will effect the exchange as rapidly as we can," she said, comfortingly. Ruth wanted to take the bag and do the swap ourselves, but the address label showed the name of a small town right down on the Belgian border. It would have taken us all day to get there, even supposing we could have found it.

Anyway, the airline rep was not about to part with another passenger's belongings.

I gave her all the possible contact numbers I could think of – Quest Tours, Philippe, the hotel where we had to pick up the Americans, even the first two galleries where we were to take them. Then Ruth and I wandered off through Customs and Immigration in a bit of a daze.

"It's not *so* bad," I said unconvincingly, pointing to our shoulder bags. "We've still got these. We've still got our money and passports and stuff."

This did not seem to comfort Ruth at all. "All my favourite clothes are in that bag," she said gloomily.

"Well, they're in good company," I said, a bit sharply. "They're with all my favourite clothes."

"You know something?" said Ruth. She stood still suddenly and fiddled with the beads in the back of her hair. I think she was afraid they might have gone missing, too. "You've always had a reputation for losing things. Even at school."

Ruth and I have been friends for seven years. I like her a lot. But that doesn't mean she never gets on my nerves.

"I've told you a million times," I said, "I do *not* lose things. Anyway you know as well as I do what happened to our case. It isn't lost – not as such."

"We don't have it any more, though, do we?" said Ruth. "As such, or not as such."

"I know that," I said, "but it's hardly my fault!"

"Not exactly, maybe," said Ruth. "But you're the one who dumped it on the conveyor belt at Heathrow. Maybe there's something about you that inspires things to get lost."

"That is *so* unfair!"

"Don't take it to heart," said Ruth. "You know what I get like when I don't feel in control of my life."

"Let's not get worked up about this," I said. I admit I sounded a bit pompous. "Let's behave like adults."

"You want me to behave like an adult?" said Ruth. "Okay, fine, I'll go start a war somewhere or dump a load of toxic chemicals in a river."

I took a deep breath and put on my most reasonable voice. "You can't be hungry," I said, "you ate on the plane. So it must be that you're tired. But just don't take it out on me . . ." My reasonable voice gave way to a mosquito-whine. ". . . I'm tired, too, and I'm getting a headache, and the short-sighted Mrs Oyting has kidnapped my aspirin, along with everything else."

"I'm sorry," said Ruth, hooking her arm through mine. "Come on, we'll head into town and track down some Dutch painkillers. My problem is that I had no idea I was so attached to possessions. I'm discovering a side of me I don't like."

By the time we reached Amsterdam Central Station we were both feeling better. My headache had gone. We had over an hour to spare. It was sunny. We knew the city was small. The map showed that we could take a route to the hotel that would take us past both the main galleries on the way. It obviously made sense to go on foot.

The first fifteen minutes went really well. We got clear of the noisy streets near the station and walked alongside canals, under trees, over bridges, past romantic-looking houseboats, and small shops with interesting window displays.

I carried the guidebook in my hand and what I thought was a clear sense of direction in my head.

We found the first gallery, exactly where we expected it to be.

Not long afterwards, we found the second gallery.

"Terrific," said Ruth. "We're back in control. Now where's the hotel?"

"On a bit," I said. "Over there. Sort of forwards and left a bit. At the edge of the centre of town – if you see what I mean."

"No," said Ruth, "I don't."

She didn't show any sign of anxiety, though, until we passed the second of the two galleries for the second time.

At first I argued that it was a different gallery.

"I recognise that oriental pot in the window," said Ruth. "And I definitely recognise that!" She pointed to a ginger cat sleeping in the doorway.

"Right," I said. "I see what I did. It's just that the bridges aren't all named on this map. Also, I was trying to go straight ahead but the canals curve round in a semi-circular shape, so you can't go straight ahead, you have to go obliquely. I get it now."

"Can I ask you a favour?" said Ruth. "Will you be totally honest with me this trip?"

"How do you mean?"

"I mean – if you get us lost, will you say so at once and not bluff."

"I've got us lost," I said.

"Thank you," said Ruth. "You may find it hard to believe, but that makes me feel better."

"I know exactly where we're trying to go," I said, defensively. "I just don't know exactly where we are."

"I'll tell you where we are," said Ruth. "We're standing outside a great-looking café. Why are we outside when we could be inside?"

It's true that I was the one who sent the case off into oblivion on the conveyor belt. However, Ruth was the one who chose the café run by the Paranoid-Depressive.

We didn't spot him straight away. He was disguised as a friendly bartender who looked a bit like a herring.

We went up to the brown wooden bar and asked him for two coffees. He indicated that we should go and sit down and turned to his coffee machine. We clumped across the brown wooden floor and sat on brown wooden chairs, at a table which had a piece of carpet as a cloth. The table was beside a window set in a brown wall. The window overlooked a canal, naturally.

Ruth, who'd paid for the coffees, dumped her shoulder-bag on the floor beside her and we looked round approvingly. It was the kind of café where people play chess, and read, and talk, and only eat and drink as a kind of afterthought.

The Paranoid-Depressive arrived at our table a couple of minutes later and put the cups in front of us. Then he pointed at the bag. "That is not wise," he said.

"I don't need a wise bag," said Ruth, startled. "I just need one that holds my stuff."

"I mean that you should guard it better," said

the P-D. "You leave it open and unconsidered on the floor and it is easy for someone to take your money."

"Oh, I see," said Ruth. She picked up the bag and dumped it the other side, between her foot and the wall. She smiled at him. "Thank you," she said.

We thought he'd go away then, but he didn't. "You are foreigners," he said, in a sombre voice. "Foreigners are always at greater risk in a city. You must take care. Amsterdam is a cultural melting pot – we have all kinds of people here – not all are good."

"It's okay," said Ruth. "We're from London. Not all the people there are good, either."

"You must be realistic about crime," said the P-D. "It would be wrong of me not to warn you to be cautious. There are pickpockets here. There are thieves. There are those who would stop at nothing to take your money and your passports. Be wary. You must understand that a British or American passport can fetch a thousand dollars."

"It's all right," I said. "We're used to travelling." I tried to sound convincing, but the P-D continued as if no one had spoken.

"Do not carry valuables in the street," he intoned. "Be careful where you walk, especially after it is dark. If you believe you are being followed, then go into a safe place. You are foreigners, you will not recognise the signs."

"This coffee smells great," said Ruth, in a bid to change the conversation.

The proprietor smiled and shrugged at us. "Trust no one," he said. Then he went back to his place behind the bar.

Ruth and I stared at each other across the carpet-cloth.

"Welcome to Amsterdam!" said Ruth.

CHAPTER FIVE

The Basilisk, Banker, Beauty Queen and Other One

I thought Ruth looked a bit down when the Paranoid-Depressive had retreated back behind his bar.

"What's the matter?" I said. "Has he rattled you?"

"He didn't exactly fill me with joyful anticipation," said Ruth, "but my main problem is culture shock."

"How do you mean?"

"I'm having trouble adjusting to the weird language everyone's using."

"They've all been speaking English."

"Exactly! Shouldn't they be talking in Dutch or Flemish or something?"

"They speak more English in Amsterdam than they do in Paris . . ." I began self-importantly.

But Ruth interrupted me.

"Paris!" she said. "Oh I feel really bad about this!"

"What?"

"Tom," said Ruth.

"I'd forgotten Tom," I said. This wasn't strictly true. It was only about ten days since we'd met him. Still, I was trying to keep cool about him. And I certainly couldn't imagine what Ruth could have to feel bad about.

"He was going to call you when he hit London."

"Is *that* all? I thought you'd remembered something serious."

"But he may be there now, and you're not!"

"Ruth, we met him twice, for about three minutes each time. He is *not* going to bother to get in touch, believe me."

"You'll probably never know, now," said Ruth gloomily, "because you won't *be* there. I should have made you check his travel dates. I was too busy thinking about Gareth. I'm sorry."

She looked so worried that I had to admit something I didn't really want to admit, even to myself. "I did check his dates," I mumbled.

"And?" said Ruth.

"It's all right, relax. I shall be safely back. I'll be there, sitting by the phone when he doesn't ring."

"You have no self-confidence at all, have you?" said Ruth.

"You can talk! After all that stuff about Gareth."

"That's different," said Ruth. "I have specific weak moments, always for a reason. Your weak moments are general – and they all join up."

"I really resent that. I'm not in the least weak."

"I don't mean you're weak. I mean your confidence is weak."

"I'm realistic," I said, "that's all. By the time Tom gets to London he'll have met dozens of other girls. He won't even remember me. *And* he'll have lost my number."

"He'll have the number," said Ruth. "*And* he'll use it." She looked so smug that for a moment I hoped he wouldn't, just to prove her wrong. But only for a moment.

Suddenly my mind clicked back into action. "I don't believe this!" I said. "We're acting as if we're on holiday. We have less than ten minutes to get ourselves into the lobby of this hotel I can't find."

"Hell fire," said Ruth, dragging her bag out from under the table and scraping her chair back. "We're losing it again. Substitute Couriers Fail To Show. And we haven't even planned what to tell them about Holland."

"We don't have to tell them anything," I said, scrabbling through the guidebook to find the street map again. "This is a Quest for Antiques Tour, not a History of The Netherlands Tour."

Fortunately, the proprietor was as good at giving directions as he was at issuing warnings. Even more fortunately, we really weren't far from the hotel.

"Boy, has this tour group drawn the short straw!" said Ruth, as we scurried into the foyer. "How shall we introduce ourselves? What about – 'Hi, we're the only couriers Quest could dig up. And we're so incompetent we can't even keep track of our own luggage.' "

"Rubbish," I said. "They'll love us. We're brilliant." To prove it, I strode up to Reception and asked them to call up two cabs straight away.

"At least we look smart," said Ruth. "Good thing we dressed to impress Philippe."

We strode confidently into the hotel lounge to pick up our group, knowing we were looking our best. Twenty-five seconds later we made an interesting and surprising discovery. It is not always a good idea to look your best.

The four Americans who were waiting for us were totally out of our class. I think we may have stared a bit, but sometimes it's hard not to. Our eyes were dazzled by designer casuals – hand-made shoes – expensive haircuts – gold jewellery. And that was just on the men.

The infuriating thing was that it would have been all right if we could have sauntered up to them in jeans and sweatshirts. Everyone knows clothes have their own language. Jeans and sweatshirts would have said, 'We could look like that if we wanted to, but frankly we don't give a damn.'

We weren't in jeans, though. Oh no. We had dressed to impress Philippe. We were colour-co-ordinated, carefully uncreased, subtly made-up. Our fashion-statement was more along the lines of 'As you can see, we've really tried – and as you can also see, we've really failed.'

I went into the introductions quickly, before I could lose my nerve. I explained that Krista, the Dutch courier, would not be escorting them after all, and that we were standing in for her.

The older of the two women, Mrs Lawrence, held out her hand and I stepped forward and shook it. "I'm sure you'll be wonderful guides," she said. Her mouth smiled widely, but her glittering, mascara-ringed eyes didn't.

Then she held forth for several minutes, telling us that the European Quest for Antiques Tour had gone well so far, and that she hoped it would continue to be as successful. It was quite clear that she was warning us that it had better be. While she talked, she somehow managed to let us know a few things – like that her husband was a high-powered banker – and that her daughter had recently won the State Beauty Contest for the second year running.

She didn't really mention the other member of the group – a young guy, expensively dressed but very ordinary-looking. Ruth and I thought he must be with the Beauty Queen. I remember I was a bit surprised she hadn't found someone more glamorous.

At that stage, and I'm really ashamed to admit this, we thought of him as the Other One. It was only partly because we hadn't been told his name. It was also because, without realising it, we were judging him by his appearance. It's impossible to explain how much I hate it when men do that to women. And however much I hate it, Ruth hates it more. But it's what we did to him. Our only excuse is that he seemed totally blank as well as ordinary. He just hung around on the edge of the group, staring into space. He didn't seem to look directly at anything, or anybody, certainly not at us.

Mr Lawrence, the Banker, looked at us all right. He looked us up and down, and smiled as if he liked what he saw. "What charming escorts," he said.

Marybeth, the Beauty Queen, looked us up and down and smiled too. Then she raised her eyebrows very slightly, changed her smile from chillingly polite to sympathetic, and gave an almost imperceptible shake of her head.

She was about our age, slim and blonde, with fingernails that exactly matched her lipstick, and lipstick that exactly matched the scarf tied jauntily in the neck of her cream silk shirt. If I tried to wear a scarf that way it would swivel round, or creep up to my ears, or come untied. On her, though, it stayed exactly as it was meant to, even when she turned her head to exchange pitying glances with her mother.

"As there are six of us, I've ordered two cars," I said loudly and hastily.

"Clever you!" said Mrs Lawrence. Somehow I knew it was not a compliment.

"We'll travel in convoy," I persisted, "so we'll all arrive at the same time."

"You're not used to doing this, are you?" said Marybeth.

"I work for Quest Tours," I said, politely, in the most non-commital voice I could manage.

"Vacation work," said Marybeth, nodding knowingly to herself. "I can tell by the tension in your voice."

Beside me, Ruth gave a tiny shudder. "I hate her," she hissed in my ear.

"Come on, then, let's go," said her mother, at the same time.

I got the family into one car. Then, as soon as Ruth and I were safely in the second car, I said, "Listen, you can go off on your own."

"And leave you at the mercy of those two?" said Ruth. "You're joking!"

"There are four of them."

"True, but the men aren't frightening. That woman's a basilisk."

"I've forgotten what a basilisk is."

"A bird whose stare can turn you to stone," said Ruth.

"I'm tougher than that," I said. "I can cope with them. What I can't cope with is keeping you under control."

"You don't have to – I'm just tagging along – I'm not your responsibility."

"Ruth, this is important. We have to be polite."

"The Dream Date isn't polite," said Ruth.

"She doesn't have to be, she's a client. Listen, you can go on a canal boat ride – you like water trips – I'll give you some guilders."

"No," said Ruth firmly. "I'll stick around. You may be able to handle the Basilisk but someone has to protect you from the Lip Gloss Princess. I suspect she has the power to destroy your limited self-confidence forever."

"Oh well, all right," I said. "But it's all going to be fine. We just have to be available for them. We won't actually have to *do* anything."

I never learn.

CHAPTER SIX

The Dipper Scam

Have you ever had the experience of seeing something but not understanding what you're seeing until it's almost too late? It happened to me in that very first gallery.

Everybody seemed to be occupied in there, apart from me and the Other One. The couple who owned the gallery were busy showing off their best antiques. They seemed to have an unlimited supply of eastern-looking pots, some on show, some which had to be brought out from behind locked doors. The Basilisk and the Beauty Queen were busy showing off their knowledge by brushing all these treasures aside on the grounds that they were not unusual enough. Twice the Basilisk said, "We want to see the best you have – we do not have a problem with finance." Ruth was admiring the view out of the window. The Banker was admiring Ruth. The Other One was pacing the floor very slowly, fitting the heel of one foot exactly against the toe of the other. Me, I was just trying to keep out of everyone's way. It was a small room and the Banker, especially, kept wandering around and colliding with people. Well, he kept colliding with me, anyhow.

The Basilisk set the oriental vase back on its stand. "This is beautiful," she said to the gallery owners, "but we already have beautiful things in our home. I'm looking for something a little more special."

Immediately, as though what she'd said had pressed a button, the gallery owners announced their intention of leading us to the other showroom, on the next floor. There, they hinted, even more wonderful things awaited our attention.

We found ourselves confronted by a flight of incredibly steep stairs. They looked almost like the companionway of a ship.

"Is there no elevator?" said the Basilisk.

"I'm afraid not," said the male half of the gallery-owning couple.

The stairs were so narrow we had to go in single file, and the Basilisk, in her tight skirt, moaned and grumbled all the way. She even took off her high heeled shoes for the last few steps. The younger ones complained less, but they still sighed a lot.

The Banker stood back graciously for me and Ruth to go ahead of him but I waved him on. I felt more in control if the group was ahead of me, and I could see it.

The Basilisk's voice floated down to us. "How they get furniture up here beats me," she said.

"There are pulleys at the tops of most of these narrow buildings," I said, in my loud, clear, tour-guide voice. "Furniture can be winched up the outside of the building and then taken in through the windows."

"Now *there's* an idea," said Ruth softly.

"Well I'm sure this place has great character," said the Basilisk, on the upper landing now, "but it is not comfortable."

Ruth snorted. "Sometimes my countrymen embarrass me," she said. "Especially Big Daddy."

"Why specially him?"

"Jo, you can be incredibly naïve," said Ruth. "Didn't you notice the way he stood back for us to go upstairs?"

"What's wrong with old-fashioned courtesy?" I said.

"There is only one reason," said Ruth, "why a man wants a woman to go up a very, very, very steep stairway ahead of him. Think about it! Also, he keeps bumping into us."

"You can't blame him for that," I said. "It's accidental."

"Like Gareth says, there are no accidents," said Ruth, through clenched teeth.

"Rubbish," I said. "And don't keep making acid remarks when we're in the room with them."

"They're not interested in what I say," said Ruth, as we reached the upper gallery. "Too busy discussing Oriental Curiosities. And tell me – why aren't they buying anything? If all they want to do is look at stuff, why aren't we taking them to museums?"

"They have to know they *can* buy if they choose to," I muttered, trying to edge Ruth into a corner behind a showcase, where her awkward remarks might be less obvious.

"Well, why don't they choose to?" said Ruth. "This stuff looks okay to me."

"Yes, but you're not the customer, are you!" I said, beginning to get irritated with her. "Hush it, will you?"

"You're getting paranoid," said Ruth. "They're not listening to me. Aren't any of these pots valuable enough, is that it? Are they holding out till they're offered something covered in gold and silver leaf?"

Then even Ruth had to accept that she could be over-heard. Marybeth, who was beside her mother on the far side of the room, turned round and said, "In fact, gold leaf isn't all that valuable. After all – people eat it."

There was a brief, surprised, pause.

At last Ruth said, "Why would they do that?"

"It's used to decorate food," said Marybeth. "In Indian Cuisine."

"Really?" said Ruth, genuinely interested now. "I've never seen that."

"You wouldn't have," said Marybeth smoothly. "I'm talking about Indian haute cuisine – not a curry takeaway."

"Oh Ruth," I said loudly and hastily, "come and look at the view from this window, it's even better than it was downstairs. See – this whole building is reflected in the canal."

For a moment I thought Ruth was going to stand her ground and say something awful. Then the Banker wandered past us to look at a silk hanging on the wall behind us. On the way he accidentally brushed against Ruth. At once she allowed me to pull her over to the window.

Marybeth gave a tiny smile and turned back to look at the dragon jar her mother was sneering at.

When Ruth and I were both at the window, our backs to the room, the tension between us faded.

It was while we were standing there, in companionable silence, that I saw the thing I didn't understand until almost too late. Perhaps I noticed because part of my mind was still wondering about the Banker, and whether or not Ruth was right about him. As I watched the people lurching by on both sides of the canal, I started to think how ungainly most humans are, how badly we move. I decided Ruth was wrong. Our Banker was genuinely clumsy. After all, why wouldn't he be? Why should he be different to the rest of the human race?

I wondered why we seemed to have such problems with our bodies. I decided perhaps it had something to do with the fact that we wear clothes and shoes. Other animals aren't clumsy. You don't see cats colliding with trees. You don't see birds making bad landings and falling off branches. You don't see dogs tripping up over the edges of paving stones – and dogs have four legs to control.

Idly, I stared down at one exceptionally clumsy man. He somehow managed to bump into a woman in a headscarf, even though there was plenty of space on the pavement for them to have passed each other easily. He obviously knew the collision was his fault. He steadied her on her feet, and I could tell by his body language that he was apologising.

He didn't learn, though. Almost as soon as he walked away from her, he collided with a man in a sludgy green anorak who had been walking towards the bridge. He didn't look to me as if he was drunk or anything – just incompetent.

Quite soon, he disappeared out of my line of vision. The green-anorak-man he had crashed into plodded off across the bridge – and blow me down if *he* didn't then collide with a *third* man, on the far side.

I started to fantasise that the first clumsy man had set off some kind of chain reaction. Maybe everyone he collided with would go off and collide with someone else, and so on. I wondered how far this could extend. By nightfall, would pairs of people in Belgium be crashing into each other?

I couldn't keep an eye on developments for long because they were all out of sight quite soon. Before I could offer my theory to Ruth, Mr Lawrence came over and put his arm lightly round my shoulders.

"We're ready to move on," he said.

The gallery owners managed to keep smiles on their faces, even though they hadn't made a sale. Ruth and I thanked them for all their help and led the way down to the door to find the cars.

Once in the street, though, our charges decided they wanted to walk. Mr Lawrence said he'd now located himself on the street map supplied by the hotel. The walk from this gallery to the next, and then back to base, didn't seem excessive to him, and they'd all like to see some local colour.

I still think they did it because they were stung by Ruth's scornful remarks. Ruth says I'm wrong. She says people like that wouldn't care what someone like her thought.

Either way, I did as I was told, paid off the drivers and watched the cars pull away. Then I did my best to keep track of my charges, who turned out to have a surprising turn of speed. I began to understand why sheepdogs look so frantic.

Suddenly, it began to rain. The people of Amsterdam expect this, and are ready for it. So at the first drop, umbrellas opened in all directions.

Even the cyclists put them up and rode with one hand for the bike and the other for the brolly.

"I should have an umbrella with me," I said to Ruth. "It's traditional."

"It certainly seems to be traditional for the Dutch and the British," said Ruth, squinting up at the clouds, "for obvious reasons."

"It is with tour guides," I said. "They hold furled umbrellas up high where they can be seen above the heads of the crowds – so the tour doesn't lose sight of them."

"You'll never believe this," said Ruth sarcastically, "but I actually thought you meant you wanted an umbrella to keep the rain off. Silly me, eh?"

"That, too," I said as we caught up with our group.

They'd dodged into a doorway to keep dry, but as we reached them the rain eased off and the two men emerged.

There was some confusion while we all ducked the passing spokes and discussed whether to shelter or keep going.

While we were in the midst of our muddle, a man hurrying past bumped into Mr Lawrence, then apologised and steadied him before moving on.

I glanced vaguely at the man as he strode by, and something stirred in my brain.

Half a second later, Mr Lawrence clutched at his chest. He was feeling for his wallet, I realised, not his heart. Being a banker, he realised instantly that he had been robbed.

In the same moment, I recognised the man who had bumped into him. It was the man I had seen collide with the woman in the headscarf.

That was when I understood what I had been seeing earlier.

I stared wildly in all directions, and there was the man in the sludgy green anorak, walking towards the nearest bridge. As I watched, the man who had dipped into Mr Lawrence's inside pocket bumped into Green-Anorak-Man. Then they both walked off in opposite directions.

It was all so fast.

As Mr Lawrence spun round to shout after the man who had collided with him, I pointed to Green-Anorak striding over the bridge and yelled, "Get him! He's passed it to him!"

Mr Lawrence took to his heels – but in pursuit of the original thief.

"It's a set-up – it's a scam!" I shrieked.

The Basilisk and her daughter stared open-mouthed.

Even Ruth's face was blank.

The Other One, though, understood exactly what I meant. He took off after Green-Anorak like a greyhound.

One more thing happened in that very crowded second of time. On the far side of the bridge a third man, until then apparently unconnected with the other two, began to run. Before that second of time was over, he was out of sight and away, never to be seen again.

CHAPTER SEVEN

Something Rare and Special

It was all annoyingly traditional. The men ran after the bad guys. The women stayed behind, and either stared or screamed, according to character.

(Ruth says I have to tell you that she didn't scream. She doesn't want her street cred destroyed forever.)

I didn't scream, either, I just yelled at people.

I yelled at the original thief to stop, which was of course pointless, but it didn't matter because the Banker caught him anyway.

I yelled at the Other One to get Green-Anorak-Man, which was pointless because he was already trying to.

Then I flung myself into the nearest shop and yelled at them to call the police. That was pointless, too, since they were already doing it, but it made me feel effective.

Mr Lawrence, who was a big man and obviously strong, hauled the original thief back towards us. He had him by the wrists, with his arms doubled up behind his back. It didn't look comfortable.

By the time they reached us, though, the thief had got his act together. He was calm. He was polite. But he was outraged. He was an innocent passer-by, he said, who had suddenly been seized and manhandled for no good reason. He was very glad, he also said, to hear the police were on their way. He was in no doubt, he went on, that they would arrest this American who had unaccountably assaulted him. He would appreciate it, he added, if someone would be good enough to search him. He would like everyone to see that he did not have the wallet.

When she'd heard all this, Mrs Lawrence instantly began to have a go at her husband. She had screamed just once, at the beginning. Now she was quiet, icy, furious.

"You've over-reacted as usual," she said. "Your wallet's probably in another pocket. What am I supposed to do if you're charged for assault in a foreign country? You expect me to visit you here in gaol, or what?"

Marybeth, who had screamed several times, began to point at something in the distance, letting out a few little extra shrieks as she did so. "Look!" she squawked, "look there!"

Obediently, we all looked across the canal to the distant figure of the Other One. He had run right across the bridge, leaving a trail of amazed pedestrians staring after him. As we watched, he grabbed Green-Anorak-Man and began to frogmarch him back across the bridge in our direction.

Marybeth turned to me. "It's your fault," she said, "you stupid cat! You made my brother go and attack that other man, and now he'll be gaoled for assault, too."

So he was her brother.

"Edward's as bad as his father," snapped Mrs Lawrence.

So he had a name.

I began to explain the dipper scam all over again. By now I had quite an audience of passers-by.

"What's a dipper?" whispered Ruth, moving closer.

"A dipper is a pickpocket," I said to the assembly, "someone who dips into your pocket – yes? Okay?"

Ruth stood still, beside me, facing the two angry women. I knew she meant to give me courage, but she had the opposite effect. I could tell she was standing by me because she, too, thought I had made a mistake. She thought something dreadful was going to happen – embarrassment, disgrace, mass arrests – and she was letting me know she was on my side.

Me? I knew I was right – but on the other hand the dipper and his team were professionals. What if they managed to talk their way out of it? What if the second man had succeeded in getting rid of the wallet? Where would that leave me?

The Basilisk, silent now, was still glaring at her husband.

Marybeth, who had managed to work herself into a state of near hysteria without her mascara smudging or her scarf slipping an inch, was still glaring at me.

Mr Lawrence, puffing with exertion, was still clinging to his quarry.

And the thief? He was smiling. He was calm. I began to get scared.

Then three things happened almost at once. The first was that the police turned up. The second was that Marybeth's brother arrived, hauling Anorak-Man with him, and approached from behind them.

The third was that Ruth glared at Marybeth and said, "Back off, will you!"

I stepped forward to speak to the two policemen, my stomach revolving like a spin drier full of feathers. The thief turned his head. Clearly, he meant to get his story in first. As he looked at the policemen, though, he saw what was right behind them – Anorak-Man in the grip of Edward. The expression on his face, and the fact that he left his mouth open but didn't say anything, helped my feathers to settle a bit. I already knew I was right, but that look proved it beyond any doubt.

Just then, I knew the thief and I had exactly the same question in our minds. Had Anorak-Man managed to pass on the wallet before the Third Man saw the commotion and legged it?

To the relief of one of us and the fury of the other, he hadn't. It was still in the inside pocket of the murky green anorak!

There followed what Ruth later called an hour and a half of intense verbal activity – most of it at the police station. They were quick about taking the statements, and they said that as both guys pleaded guilty there wouldn't be any need for any of us to turn up at the trial. They also dished out quite a lot of praise in my direction. Ruth said she was proud of me. Mr Lawrence said he was deeply grateful.

Me, I was embarrassed. I was quite relieved when I realised that none of this meant that the two female Lawrences were going to start being nice to me. I'm not sure I could have handled that.

Nothing had changed, though. In spite of the fact that everything had ended well, this was not the way they had planned to spend their morning, and the Basilisk was careful to let us know this.

By the time we eventually reached the second gallery we were in some disarray. The Basilisk and the Beauty Queen were sulky and snappish because they'd been wrong and I'd been right. They were also complaining that the brief rainstorm had ruined their hair. The Banker was in mega-hugging-mode because he was so pleased with us for saving all his dosh. Ruth was getting dangerously ratty. I heard her say, "Okay, so you're pleased, just tell me, don't get physical." I was trembly with shock and relief.

Edward had switched back into remote-mode and seemed to be doing his best to keep clear of the lot of us. He was the only one who'd understood me when I was yelling about Green Anorak-Man. Just for a few minutes back there we'd been a team. Glancing at him, I could see that was now in the forgotten past.

The six of us got ourselves into the gallery in a state of irritable confusion. Once there, though, things changed totally – and not only because of the calm ginger cat who strode forward to greet us as we went in.

This gallery was run by a tall fair-haired woman who spoke the same perfect English everyone else had spoken. She showed us the best of her stock right away.

"I know you are especially interested in Oriental Antiquities," she said, "and so I thought perhaps this . . ."

She led us to a table at the back of the downstairs room and indicated something amazing that stood on it. For a few moments no one said anything, we all just stared.

It was a golden statuette, about two feet high, of a young and beautiful Buddha. He stood upright, his eyes lowered, his mouth in a slight smile. One slim hand was raised, palm up, to the sky. The other hand was lowered, palm down, towards the ground. In the centre of his forehead a blue stone gleamed.

"It's 15th or 16th century Tibetan," said the blonde woman. "Gilded bronze and very heavy. See how he stands – so that he is the medium of communication between heaven and earth?"

Still no one spoke. He was just so beautiful, so delicately made, and his expression was so peaceful and so gentle that it seemed impossible to look away from him.

When she mentioned the price it seemed meaningless. I did a quick calculation and realised she was asking thousands of pounds for him, but while I was actually looking at him I could see that he was worth whatever money anyone had, plus some.

Mr Lawrence put his hand out as though to touch the Buddha, but then withdrew it again as if he didn't quite like to. Mrs Lawrence, who had examined and questioned every single thing she'd been shown in the first gallery, stood quietly with her hands folded. Marybeth was quiet, too, half leaning against her mother, staring. Even Edward joined the group instead of pacing around as far away as possible.

Ruth breathed in my ear, "Isn't that something? I almost think I can see an aura around it."

"I wouldn't be surprised if you could," I whispered back.

Neither of us was whispering because of the Lawrences or because of the gallery owner. It wouldn't have mattered if they'd heard. We were whispering – and this may sound odd – but we were whispering the way you might whisper in church.

"The price may seem high," said the gallery owner, perhaps thinking that was what had caused the silence, "but the jewel in the forehead is a sapphire. Also, so far as we can possibly tell, the figure is unique. It was bought in Tibet by a purchaser who had been assured that the craftsman who fashioned it only made one such piece in his life. It was brought back to Europe some twenty years ago, but only came on the market about five years ago. Since then it has changed hands several times. We were lucky to acquire it."

"We'll take it," said Mrs Lawrence at last, and Mr Lawrence joined in at the end of her sentence . . . "Take it, yes," he said.

We stood round in respectful silence while all kinds of paperwork was dealt with.

As the statue was quite large and heavy, the blonde woman offered to package it and send it over to the States to await the Lawrences' return. However, they refused to walk out of the gallery without it. So she agreed to sort out the necessary export permit with the Dutch authorities and have the permit delivered to the hotel by lunch time next day. She was clearly extremely efficient.

I tried to match her efficiency by asking to use her phone to call two cabs to take us back to the hotel. The Lawrences wouldn't hear of it, though. They had decided to take in some local colour and nothing would change their minds.

I did my best. I planted myself in front of Mr Lawrence and said, "Look, walking is a really bad idea. We've already had problems, and now you have something truly valuable with you."

"Our problems are over," said Mr Lawrence, "thanks to you. It'll be fine. I insist."

What more could I do?

Before long, we were all processing out of the gallery, still silent, still unusually calm. We set off in single file, at a slow, almost ceremonial pace, led by the Banker and the Buddha. Ruth and I followed at the rear of the column.

We'd only gone a few yards when Ruth said, "I wish you'd stop looking over your shoulder, you're making me nervous."

"Sorry," I said. "I just get the feeling we're being followed."

"Forget it," said Ruth. "The cops've got them banged up."

"It isn't them," I said.

"Who then?" said Ruth, looking back.

"I don't know. Someone else."

"There are all kinds of people cruising around," said Ruth, "but no one's interested in us. Relax. It isn't far."

I was still uneasy. I forced myself to look straight ahead for the length of a street. Then I spun round suddenly. I thought if I did that I might catch them at it – whoever they were and whatever they were doing.

I tried this technique several times, with limited success.

"What is it?" said Ruth.

"I'm just so sure we're being followed," I said. "I'm sure I keep seeing the same person behind us. But there are so many other people around it's hard to get more than a glimpse."

"So what do you think you glimpse?"

"A man in a shabby old coat, rather long. And a bit further back there's someone else who keeps crossing the road and then crossing back. I *think* it's always the same person – a man in a blue denim jacket."

"Hang on," said Ruth. "You're saying there are two of them?"

"I'm not sure what I'm saying, but I definitely think there's something going on behind us."

"You paid too much attention to the guy in the brown café," said Ruth. "Forget him."

"It isn't because of him," I said. "At least I don't think it is. I just have a feeling about this – there's someone back there – maybe two someones."

"Come on!" said Ruth. "You've already single-handedly stamped out the Amsterdam crime wave. You don't have to do any more. You're imagining it."

I wasn't, though.

CHAPTER EIGHT

The Beginnings of Anxiety

It wasn't a long walk back to the hotel. The weight of the Buddha slowed Mr Lawrence down, though, so it took a while. The rest of the family walked silently behind him, in single file. It seemed that they were still calmed by the sense of peace the statue had given out.

However, the calm was beginning to wear off at the back of the line, where Ruth and I walked, trying not to look over our shoulders.

"You were in a funny mood even before we left," said Ruth. "Back in London you thought that supermarket guard was following us."

"Well, he was."

"Only because he was wondering if we were the people who'd abandoned poor, ill-treated George," said Ruth. "That deprived child who'd actually had to pick up some groceries by himself."

"It was nothing to do with that," I said. "He thought we were potential shoplifters. He had us under surveillance. I think he was planning to stop us at the door and hold us for questioning."

"So why didn't he?"

"Because he and George had bonded over the icing sugar. As soon as he realised we were all George had, he decided to let us leave with him."

"Nah," said Ruth, "I don't think he suspected us of anything. He probably wasn't even following us. He probably just happened to be walking the same way. You have too much imagination."

"I wonder why I like you?" I said. "You can be so annoying. Are you saying the pickpocket thing was all in my mind? If so, I must have impressive powers of persuasion. The entire Lawrence family and a contingent of Dutch police joined in my fantasy – remember?"

"You did brilliantly," said Ruth, "you were a star. I still don't know how you figured it out."

"Don't forget, Dad and I often go bird-watching," I said, feeling a bit better. "That teaches you to be observant." I looked over my shoulder again.

"My point," said Ruth, "is that you don't have to go on being so observant."

"Tour guides have to be vigilant," I said. "That's not unreasonable. Rich people *do* get followed by thieves – we know that."

"Lightning doesn't strike in the same place twice," said Ruth.

"Forget it!" I said. "There's a man in Virginia who's been struck seven times. And let's face it, they do look rich. Designer casuals, handmade shoes."

"You mentioned handmade shoes before," said Ruth. "How can you tell? Have they got fingerprints on them or what?"

The hotel was actually in sight on the far side of the road, when we were temporarily split up. The

pedestrian lights allowed Mr and Mrs Lawrence and
Marybeth to get across. Then they changed abruptly,
leaving the Other One, Edward the Silent, stranded
at the edge of the pavement. Ruth and I caught up
with him and the three of us stood in a row and
waited our turn.

I noticed Edward turn his head and look back the
way we'd come. I waited until a particularly noisy
tram had racketed past us, and then said reassuringly,
"It's all right, we haven't lost the others. They're
ahead of us. Look – they're just going into the hotel
now."

"Yeah, I know," said Edward. It was the first time
he'd spoken. I was almost surprised to find that he
could. "I just wondered . . ." He looked me straight
in the eye. "Do you get the feeling we're being followed," he said, "or am I paranoid?"

"I've thought it ever since we left the gallery,"
I said amazed. All three of us turned and stared
searchingly along the road that stretched out behind
us. So searchingly, in fact, that we missed our next
chance at the lights. "I never really get a good look,
though, so I can't be sure."

"If he's that hard to pick out," said Edward,
"sounds like he's a professional – which is bad news."

"On the other hand," said Ruth, "you could say
the fact that you've spotted him at all means he's an
amateur."

"I guess that theory works, too," said Edward, and
he almost smiled.

"Are you a banker, too?" said Ruth.

"No – I'm in veterinary college," said Edward.

"What should I do about it?" I said. Half of me

was pleased that I wasn't the only one who thought we were being tailed. The other half was beginning to get the creeps about whoever was behind us.

"You don't have to do anything about it," said Ruth. "Edward does the studying, Edward cures the animals."

"You know what I mean! About our follower."

The lights changed and we ran across the road.

"It's been a funny kind of day," said Ruth, "you probably are imagining it – both of you."

"Jo's powers of observation are pretty slick," said Edward. "That dipper scam is notoriously hard to spot. But I don't see what we can do, right now – except get the statue locked away somewhere secure."

Because Mr Lawrence had been walking slowly with his burden, we caught up with the other three in the lobby almost before they realised we'd been left behind. It was a huge relief to be safely inside the enormous, busy, efficient-looking hotel. Even so, I didn't relax properly until Mr Lawrence had stowed the Buddha in the manager's safe.

As soon as he'd done that he stopped being quiet and dreamy and became flamboyant again. I realised he'd been nervous, too. Probably they all had. The statue was a serious investment, even for the rich.

He strode up to us and flung one arm around Ruth's shoulders and the other round mine.

"Now!" he said. "I insist that both our beautiful guides join us for lunch."

"Excuse me," said Ruth. She ducked out from under his arm and moved a couple of feet away.

Mr Lawrence looked faintly surprised and tightened his grip on me.

"I insist," he repeated. "It's the least I can do. After all, you saved more than the price of everyone's lunch when you spotted that second guy." He looked across at his family. "Tell them they have to join us," he beamed.

I looked across at his family, too. Edward was smiling and nodding – not at me specially, at both of us. Mrs Lawrence and Marybeth, though, were standing side by side, neither smiling nor nodding. They were staring at the banker in such disbelief that I actually felt sorry for them.

Before they had time to embarrass us all by saying what they thought of the idea, I wriggled free of the encircling arm. Then I swept the whole company with my most winning smile, and said that it was a lovely invitation, but that unfortunately Ruth and I had business to attend to. We would escort them to the restaurant of their choice, I continued, and then return for them in an hour and a half to take them to the Spiegelkwartier, where they could continue their Quest for Antiques among its shops and galleries.

Mr Lawrence looked crestfallen. Edward shrugged slightly and moved away from the group the way he had before – fitting the heel of each foot against the toe of the other.

Without particularly meaning to, the Basilisk made the next bit easy for us.

"I think we should have lunch right here, in the hotel coffee shop," she said. "I'm exhausted. And give us two hours, will you. Marybeth and I both need to visit the beauty parlour to repair the damage done by that rainstorm."

Marybeth glanced over at the hotel's hairdressing salon, which led off the lobby opposite the coffee shop. "I just hope they can fit us in," she said. She gave me a fierce, glittering smile, nearly as alarming as her mother's, and added, "It's a pity you didn't call ahead and fix it up for us."

"I'm sorry," I said. I was cross with myself for not thinking of that. I'd heard them complain about their hair earlier – I should have picked up on it. "I'll go and check with them now."

"Our French courier didn't have to be prompted to do things like that," remarked Mrs Lawrence.

"Hey!" said Mr Lawrence, "give the kids a break – they were busy catching thieves for us, they can't do everything."

"That's true," said Marybeth sweetly – too sweetly. "And you can see they don't use professional beauty care themselves, so it isn't the kind of thing they'd think of."

Mr Lawrence beamed at his daughter for being so understanding. Me? I grabbed the strap of Ruth's shoulder bag and towed her over to the salon reception with me, before she had a chance to respond.

"I'll deck her," she was muttering, as I made two urgent and immediate appointments. "At the end – after you sign off – I swear I'll deck her."

Three minutes later, she and I walked out of the hotel. The Buddha was in the safe. The women were in the salon. The men were in the bar. I felt a huge sense of relief.

Even so, I had a good look round before we walked away. I was willing to accept that I might have been wrong about there being two people following us –

but I was absolutely certain there had been one. So, I now knew, was Edward.

I saw no sign of shadowy figures, though, and decided whoever it was had given up. He was probably put off because there were so many of us – and he would never invade that huge, plush hotel.

Or so I thought.

CHAPTER NINE

The Pursuer Closes In

"It's a good thing," said Ruth, as we headed down the street, "that we didn't tell them what we really have to do now – find our missing luggage and hope to get a place to stay over. I think we could lose points."

I'd been so keen to get away that I hadn't thought to use the payphone in the hotel, so we had to look for one in the street.

"Can I ask you a personal question?" said Ruth. "Are you interested in Ed the Vet?"

"No," I said, "why?"

"You kind of keep looking at him," said Ruth.

"Do I?" I said, startled. "Has anyone else noticed?"

"Doubt it."

"It's just that he's so quiet. I can't help wondering what he's thinking."

"I know what you mean," said Ruth. "Is he shy or is he bored? Tell you what I think, I think you should flirt with him."

"What!"

"You're always telling me you're no good at attracting men. So – practise on Edward."

"Ruth, that's awful. He *is* a human being."

"That's why I suggested it," said Ruth. "Not much future in flirting with a racoon."

"Here's a callbox," I said sternly.

"If the bag's there," said Ruth, letting go of her unnerving suggestion, "do we have time to go out and collect it?"

"Let's see what they offer," I said. "They might agree to send it to the Lawrences' hotel on the airport bus or something."

"Great!" said Ruth. "I can't wait to get my stuff back."

She had to, though. Mrs Oyting had not, after all, rushed back to Schipol to make the switch. Nor was anyone answering the phone at the address on the label.

The airline rep was as reassuring as she'd been before. In her experience, she repeated, luggage lost in this way was always reunited with its true owner.

"What's wrong with that woman," said Ruth, when I'd passed on this news, "doesn't she like her own clothes, or what?"

"I'm sure we'll get it back by tonight," I said uneasily.

"We'd better!" said Ruth.

"There's still the whole afternoon and evening," I said, trying to sound as reassuring as the airline rep. "I think we should go straight to the Tourist Office now, and find somewhere to stay."

Ruth agreed – but she thought we should eat lunch

first. This seemed reasonable, especially as the guide-book told us we were near a good canalside café.

We sat outside and ordered savoury pancakes the size of dinner plates from a typically Dutch waiter – young, smiling, blond.

"This bit's all right, anyway," said Ruth enthusi-astically, as he strolled away again, swinging his tray from one hand.

"I'm sorry about this diversion," I said. "We'll be in Paris by tomorrow night."

"Oh, I'm not complaining," said Ruth. "I'm having a good time. I like it here – despite being patronised by a rich kid and groped by her father."

"He did not grope you!"

"Maybe not yet," said Ruth, "but he's working up to it."

"You're over-reacting."

"I tell you," said Ruth, pointing at me with a fork-ful of pancake, "if he invades my space one more time you'll all find out what overreacting can *really* be like."

"You can go off on your own," I said sternly. "I told you before."

"Don't worry," said Ruth, "I won't embarrass you. I'll just keep clear of him."

As soon as our plates were empty, the typically Dutch waiter wandered back and said, "You guys want dessert?"

The typically Dutch waiter, it turned out, was American. He sat down with us for a few minutes, and chatted, while we ran through all the possible puddings and then settled on two coffees.

It turned out he knew someone who ran a small

hotel, really cheap, more of a hostel in fact – and ideal for our situation. I was a little unsure, but Ruth was bubbling with enthusiasm, so I just drank my coffee while he made a phone call and then wrote down the address for us.

It was a bit further away than we'd expected, but we managed it without having to brave public transport. Then we stood outside for a while, considering.

Ruth said she thought maybe I didn't like the look of the place because my glimpses of the high-tech splendour of the Lawrences' hotel had turned my head.

"It's cheap," she said. "That's what we wanted."

"It's at the edge of the Red Light district," I said. "It is *not* in a nice area."

"It's only for one night," said Ruth, and she bounded up the steps and into the narrow hall.

An elderly man appeared from a room somewhere deep inside the building and came to greet us.

He seemed to think the decision had already been made.

"You want to check in now?" he said.

"We don't have our luggage with us yet," began Ruth.

I could tell she was planning to explain the situation to him, but he stopped her.

"No problem," he said. "I show you the room."

He set off up the stairs and, obediently, we followed.

"It's okay," Ruth whispered to me. "Not fancy, maybe, but okay."

She was right about it not being fancy.

The elderly man unlocked the door of a room and

stood back for us to go in ahead of him. It had two beds in it and nothing much else. There were curtains at the windows but I wasn't convinced they would stay up if anyone tried to pull them across.

"We are not in the best part of town here," said the elderly man with endearing honesty. "But that is why my rooms are so reasonable. You will not have en suite facilities, either. But . . ." he backed out of the open door and pointed down the corridor, ". . . there are facilities, behind that door at the end. And as we are not in the best part of town, I advise you to leave your valuables in your room here. Do not carry them through the streets. The door has a good lock."

Ruth and I opened our mouths at the same moment.

Ruth was going to say, "We'll take it."

I was going to say, "We'll let you know." Then I was going to leave and never come back.

Before either of us could say anything, though, he handed Ruth the key, smiled, turned his back on us, and set off down the stairs.

We stood and stared at each other for a moment. Then I began to examine the beds. "The sheets look clean," I said. "I think."

"So what do we do?" said Ruth.

"We may as well stay," I said, a bit reluctantly. "You're right, it's only for one night, and it saves hoofing around to find somewhere else."

"I assumed we were staying," said Ruth. "I meant – what do we do about valuables? Leave them in the room or take them with us?"

"We haven't exactly got much to worry about," I said, "at the moment."

"Money," said Ruth. "And passports. Don't forget the Paranoid-Depressive in the Brown Café. According to him they're worth a thousand dollars each."

"We've been carrying them all day," I said. "Why stop now?"

"Because we're at the bad end of town," said Ruth. "We have to walk through the mean streets before we hit the classy bit."

I hesitated. "What did you think of the manager?" I said.

"He seemed okay."

"But he's got a master-key, hasn't he? Must have. Do you think he might have wanted to panic us into leaving stuff so he could come in and nick it?"

"Could be," said Ruth. "I think we should take it all with us. We're going to look really stupid if we leave it behind and it isn't here when we get back. Think of trying to explain to the cops. Well, Officer, we left our stuff in our room in a dodgy hotel because a seedy looking man with a pass key said we should."

"But we're not going to look any brighter if we take it with us and get mugged for it," I said. "Then we'd have to say, yes, Constable, we were warned to leave it locked into our room but we preferred to carry it around the back alleys with us."

"Here's another thought, though," said Ruth. "What if we don't take the stuff and we get mugged anyway? If they find nothing to steal they'll probably stab us in rage."

"That sounds more like New York than Amsterdam."

71

"You're telling me there are no knives in Holland?" said Ruth.

"Suppose we split the difference?" I said. "How about one of us leaves her stuff here and the other carries hers with her? Then, whichever way it goes, at least one of us will have money. And at least one of us will have a passport as proof of identity if we have to go to the police to report the other lot stolen. What do you think?"

"I think I'll sell my own passport," said Ruth. "I could use a thousand bucks."

"I wish we'd never started this conversation," I said. "I can't move now. I'll never be able to leave this room."

"Okay," said Ruth, decisively, "let's each make our own decision. I tell you what I'm going to do. I'm going to take my stuff with me. Not because I think it'll be any safer, but because I can't stand the suspense of wondering what's happened to it. Worrying about the baggage is all I can handle right now."

That made sense. So that was what we did.

We had nearly forty-five minutes in hand before we had to pick up the Lawrences, so we took our time. We even managed a quick walk through the open air market. Ruth bought a tub of assorted olives – more different kinds than I've ever seen before – and we ate them as we walked.

"Very Dutch!" I said. "We're surrounded by cheeses and Delft china windmills and clog fridge magnets and you pick Greek olives!"

"Sorry," said Ruth, "but I can't manage a whole cheese and the fridge magnets looked indigestible. Try one of these big green ones, they're magic."

By the time we got back to the hotel, we were both in a really good mood. All we needed now, I thought, was news from the airline that our luggage was on its way to us and everything would be perfect.

In fact I felt so hopeful about this that I didn't lead the way straight to the coffee shop. First I went up to the reception desk and asked if there'd been a message for us.

There hadn't. I explained we weren't staying there, but that we'd given the number to the airline. The receptionist was really nice and said that a message would certainly have been taken for us if one had come through. But none had.

Neither of us felt quite as cheerful, when we turned away from the desk, as we had when we'd strolled in two minutes earlier.

I felt even less cheerful when I caught sight of someone walking, slowly and cautiously, through the archway that led from the lobby to the coffee shop. The figure was familiar, because I'd seen it before. At the same time it was unfamiliar, because I hadn't seen it clearly till now.

It was the figure of a man in a shabby old coat, rather long. It was the figure of the man who had been tailing us ever since we left the gallery carrying the gilded bronze Buddha.

CHAPTER TEN

A Good Story

By the time Ruth and I reached the coffee shop entrance, the man in the long shabby coat was already inside. He was making his way towards a table in the far corner where the four members of the unsuspecting Lawrence family were sitting.

"It's definitely him," I said to Ruth. "That's the man who was following us, I'm sure."

"Well, he's out in the open now," said Ruth. "He's going right up to them."

"Come on," I said. I told myself there was no need to feel nervous inside this busy hotel. "We'd better help them give him the brush-off."

He reached their table before us, and by the time we got there Mrs Lawrence was already making a discreet shoo-ing gesture in his direction. Mr Lawrence, rather more surprisingly, was fishing change out of his pocket and looking through it.

"Oh, I see," said Ruth quietly, "he's a beggar."

"Hello," I said firmly, to the group in general. I had decided that if I started confidently I'd be better able to sort out whatever it was that was happening.

"We're here to take you on the second part of your Quest Tour."

"Good," said Mrs Lawrence, looking sharply at her watch. I think she was hoping to be able to tell us we were late. We weren't, though, so she couldn't.

Mr Lawrence selected some coins and held them out.

The shabby man kept his own hands at his sides and shook his head. "No, no," he said, "I am not asking for money, I assure you. Though I am a suppli-cant, of sorts."

He smiled politely at the group at the table and then turned slightly so that his smile included us. "My name is Karel," he said. "I do not wish to inconvenience anyone, but I have travelled a long way. May I beg just a few moments of your time?"

He had a quiet voice, with an accent I couldn't place. It was hard to tell what age he was. He might have been fifty, or he might have been much older. From close to it was possible to see that although he was shabby, and although his coat looked as if it belonged to someone taller, he didn't seem to be a tramp. He didn't seem to be mad, either. Just out of place in these ultra-smart surroundings.

"I'm sorry," said Mrs Lawrence curtly, and she pushed her chair back, ready to get up. "We have no time."

"What do you want?" said Mr Lawrence. He seemed more puzzled than curious. I don't expect he was used to having his dollars refused.

"I would like to explain to you about the Buddha," said Karel.

Edward leant forward across the table. "Did you follow us from the gallery?" he said.

"Yes," said Karel.

Edward, Ruth and I exchanged glances. So two of us had been right.

"Come on, let's go," said Marybeth, nudging her mother.

"What do you mean – you want to explain about the Buddha?" said Edward.

"I want to explain that I would like to buy it back from you," said Karel simply. "But I fear I can only offer less than half the sum you gave for it."

That threw us all into confusion.

Mrs Lawrence and Marybeth clearly didn't want to hear any more. Karel's presence seemed to unsettle them and being unsettled made them cross. Also, they were ready to go shopping again.

Ruth and I were uneasy, and Edward looked puzzled. Mr Lawrence, though, was intrigued – so much so that he got up and dragged over two spare chairs from the empty table beside him, and signed for Ruth and me to sit down.

"We'll hear your story," he said to Karel – who was not offered a seat. Then, before they had a chance to object, he shook his head at his wife and daughter and said, "It won't take a minute. I'd like to hear someone try to convince me to go for such an obviously bad deal."

"Thank you," said Karel. "What I wish you to know is that until a very few years ago the Buddha was ours."

"Yours?" said Mr Lawrence. "So who are you?"

"We are a small monastic community, based in Germany."

"Buddhist monks, you mean?" said Edward.

"We are closer to Buddhism than to any other major religion," said Karel, "but we believe that an honest search for truth will always achieve its end, whatever route is taken."

"And what route do you take?" said Mr Lawrence.

"We withdraw from the distractions of the world, we seek stillness, we practise meditation, we pass on our teaching if it is asked for. We do not use money. We rely on what we grow and on the honey from our bees. From time to time people come to us on retreat – some for a few days, some for weeks – and in exchange for the peace we offer they give us food, or the use of their skills to keep our buildings in repair."

"Now wait a minute, here," said Mr Lawrence. "You say this very valuable statue used to be yours – well how come? If you have no money, how did you get it?"

"Our founder was a rich man," said Karel, "who achieved enlightenment suddenly, and late in life. Then he gave away his worldly goods to become a hermit and teacher. Later, gradually, the rest of us joined him. The Buddha-statue, which he bought for the community, used up the last of his worldly wealth. He believed that it expressed everything that man needs to know. He believed that the very sight of it brought peace to the human mind."

Mr Lawrence frowned and nodded. "That's true enough," he said, "it does." He looked round at the rest of us. "Doesn't it?" he added.

Some of us nodded – but the Basilisk and the Beauty Queen were not among them.

"None of this is of any interest to us," said Mrs Lawrence. "The statue is ours, bought and paid for, and it isn't for sale."

"Hold your horses," said Mr Lawrence, "if it really belongs to these guys, I want to know . . ."

"It doesn't!" said Mrs Lawrence. "It belongs to us." She looked directly at Karel for the first time. "If you know so much about it," she said, "where is it from?"

"It is from Tibet," said Karel. "It was created in the 15th century by a great master who put all his wisdom into it. It was discovered there by a collector and dealer some twenty years ago. He brought it back to Europe and it was there that our founder discovered it and bought it."

"That sounds plausible," said Edward softly, glancing at his mother.

She made an impatient gesture which I translated to mean 'so what'. "I imagine your 'founder' was too unworldly to ask for a receipt when he bought it from this dealer!" she said dismissively.

"He was a wise man," said Karel, reaching into an inside pocket and taking out a slip of paper. "He understood the workings of the world. He acquired a receipt, and it was kept, because we thought someone might challenge our right to the Buddha-statue, believing us to be too poor to own such a thing."

He handed the piece of paper to Mr Lawrence, who read it, nodded, and passed it around the table.

"It was our only valuable possession – but for us its value lies in its teaching powers, not in its monetary worth," said Karel. "However, we understand that others value it differently which is why we understand that our only chance of recovering it is if we buy it back. I have been pursuing it for five years, now, and the price continues to rise beyond the money I have. But still I must try – and so I am here, with little hope, to try to buy it back from you."

Mr Lawrence turned to look at his wife. "It's theirs all right," he said, pointing to the piece of paper which was now in her hand. "It's described well enough on that."

Mrs Lawrence passed the receipt on so it completed its circuit of the table, ending up with me. "Anyone could have written that out," she said. "It's meaningless."

"It speaks to me," said Mr Lawrence. "I mean, think about it. Whoever made that statue, back in the fifteenth century, didn't mean it to end up on a coffee table somewhere."

"Whoever made it and whatever he made it for," said Mrs Lawrence, slowly and forcefully, "and whoever did or didn't once own it, is not our problem. We bought it in good faith. It's ours. Ours to keep."

"We can't keep something as an ornament that has such spiritual significance," said Mr Lawrence. "We may have paid money for it, but morally it belongs to the monastery."

With a bit of a shock, I realised that the Banker, the hard-headed businessman, had fallen for the story in a big way. I realised something else, too. While Karel was actually speaking, in his soft hypnotic voice, so had I.

I felt I ought to say something, but I didn't know

what. I stared at the bit of paper. How could I tell if it was genuine or not? I looked at Ruth and she gave me a helpless look back.

"Now just a moment," said Mrs Lawrence. She had obviously been shaken by her husband's reaction, too, and had decided to take charge. She gave Karel the full force of her basilisk stare. "No need to ask why you chose to persecute us with this tale!" she said. "No need to ask why you didn't go direct to the gallery! You obviously decided naïve Americans would be a soft touch. Well, you're very wrong."

Karel didn't flinch under the stare. "I did approach the gallery," he said simply. "As soon as I had tracked the Buddha-statue there. They turned me down."

"*What* a surprise," said Mrs Lawrence.

Karel shrugged. "They are a commercial venture," he said. "They have a living to make." He smiled at me and held out his hand for the receipt. I handed it back to him.

"If the thing means so much to you," said Edward, "how did you manage to lose it?"

"It was taken away from us," said Karel, putting the receipt carefully back into his pocket.

"Stolen?" said Edward.

"It was taken by someone who came to us on retreat. I don't think he planned to do it. I think he was unexpectedly tempted."

"Perhaps you shouldn't have had something so valuable," said Edward. "Perhaps you shouldn't have had such temptation around?"

"In other words," said Mrs Lawrence sharply, "weren't you asking for it?"

"Hey," said Mr Lawrence, "there's no call to be offensive."

Karel didn't look in the least offended. "If there is no temptation," he said, "how can anyone resist it, and grow?"

"Where did you keep it?" said Mr Lawrence. He was hooked. You could see he was hooked. "On an altar, perhaps?"

"Not an altar. Just a shelf. In our meditation room."

Marybeth had been working up to saying something for several minutes. Now she exploded with, "It's just a pagan idol that happens to look good, that's all. It'll look great on our hall table, where we are going to put it. They can get some other idol if they want." Because Karel didn't interrupt her, she got pushier. "It is an idol, isn't it?" she said to him.

It was perfectly obvious that she was trying to insult him. It was also obvious that he didn't feel insulted.

"As I understand the word," he said thoughtfully, "an idol is something that is worshipped. We do not worship the Buddha-statue. We use it as an aid to meditation. Those who are truly advanced have no need of it, of course, but most of us appreciate a little help."

"I think I understand," said Mr Lawrence, nodding.

"You do not," said Mrs Lawrence. "You know nothing about it."

"Well, at least I know I don't know," said Mr Lawrence sharply. "At least I'm willing to learn."

"You're in the process of being conned," said his

wife. "I'm amazed you can't see that. He admits he followed us from the gallery. This is his profession. He hangs around till someone buys something valuable and then he tails them and comes up with whatever story seems likely to work."

"He's offering to *buy* it," said Mr Lawrence.

"For less than half its value," said Mrs Lawrence. "Then he'll sell it for full value, or more." She turned to Karel. "Was it insured?" she snapped.

"We have no money for such things," said Karel.

"If an insurance agent came on retreat," interrupted Edward, "wouldn't you accept insurance of the statue as his gift to the community?"

"No insurance agent has ever come on retreat, so I can't answer that."

"Right," said Mrs Lawrence triumphantly. "If you got no insurance pay-out, where did you get the money you're offering us?"

"The man who took the Buddha sold it," said Karel. "I don't know that he sold it very wisely, because he knew only that it was valuable, not how valuable it was, and he didn't know the right places to go. However, after some months, he felt so bad about what he had done that he returned all the money to the community. It is this money that I have to offer."

"I don't know that I'm going to take your money," said Mr Lawrence softly. "But I do know that I'm going to return your statue."

I happened to be looking at Karel as he said this, but his expression was unreadable. I suppose I thought a con man would have looked triumphant at that moment, but that was silly of me. If Karel was a con artist he was a good one. He wouldn't slip up at the last moment.

"I would insist that you took the money," he said, "such as it is. We have no other use for it."

I reached out and caught at Mr Lawrence's arm. "You should think about this," I said. "It's too big a decision to make so quickly."

"I've been judging people all my working life," said Mr Lawrence. "And I've never been wrong. This guy is straight, I know it."

"In your working life you judge people with your head," said Mrs Lawrence. "You're using your heart, now."

She and her daughter were thoroughly agitated by now, but Mr Lawrence, who had been gazing steadily at Karel all this time, was growing visibly calmer. Now he laughed. "Don't be so scornful about my heart," he said to his wife. "I used it to choose you!"

"Can we telephone this monastery?" said Edward.

"We have no telephone," said Karel.

"So how do people arrange to come on retreat?"

"They write. Or they simply arrive."

"Do you have neighbours we can call?" I suggested. "Is there a police station nearby, or a hotel, or something?"

"The monastery is in the mountains in Germany, near the border with the Czech Republic. It is very remote. We have no neighbours."

"That's very convenient," said Mrs Lawrence acidly.

I'm certain Karel understood what she meant, but he answered innocently, "No, as a matter of fact it is often very inconvenient."

Mr Lawrence rose to his feet. "This is a big moment for me," he said. "I've never had a chance to do anything like this in my life before. I *will* return your statue. Maybe one day I can visit your retreat?"

"You would be most welcome," said Karel.

"I'm so grateful that I was the one to buy it," said Mr Lawrence. He was in quite an emotional state, in fact he sounded embarrassingly close to tears. "It will be a privilege to do the right thing," he went on. "I'll go and fetch it."

Mrs Lawrence stood up, too. "Just hang on," she said, "don't I get a say?"

"Look," said Edward, "this really isn't something to be discussed in a hotel coffee shop – if we're not careful we'll get an audience. Let's go up to your suite, Pop, and talk there."

"Right!" said Mr Lawrence. "I'll go get it from the safe. You take Karel up." And he strode off before any of us could speak.

I was very nervous at the thought of the statue coming out of its safe place, but if his family couldn't stop the Banker, I certainly couldn't. At least Edward's suggestion gave us all a bit more time – and it got his father away from Karel's hypnotic voice for a few minutes.

Mrs Lawrence signed to Ruth and me that we should follow. Then she, Marybeth and Edward went on ahead, talking urgently. Karel followed at a respectful distance. Ruth and I trailed along last.

"What do you think?" said Ruth.

"I think I wish we were in Paris," I said.

"That Karel's pretty convincing," said Ruth. "If he is bluffing, then he's a very good bluffer."

"Con men *are* good bluffers," I said.

"So you don't believe him?"

"The stupid thing is," I said, "that I think I do. But how can I know if I'm right or not? Also, I've got something else to tell you that you won't like."

"What?"

We were in the lobby by now. The three Lawrences were in the large lift, standing at one side. Karel was standing at the other side. Edward was holding the door for us. I hadn't much time. "Over there, by Reception," I said. "See that man with his back to us, looking at the postcard rack?"

"The one in the blue denim jacket?" said Ruth.

"Yes."

"What about him?"

"You know I said I thought there might be two people tailing us when we left the gallery? Well, he looks exactly like the second one."

CHAPTER ELEVEN

An Unexpected Sighting

The lounge of the Lawrences' suite was enormous and there seemed to be mirrors on every wall. I caught sight of myself in one almost as soon as I walked in. My subtle make-up had vanished, my hair needed brushing and I looked totally spaced out. I glanced at Ruth. She had the same three problems.

"At least we don't look creased," I said quietly.

"You can always depend on modern fabric technology," said Ruth.

It had been a long day. Also it had become slightly surreal. If anyone had stopped me in the airport at dawn and asked what Ruth and I would be doing at three that afternoon I'd have found it easy to make a few guesses. Drinking coffee in a Paris restaurant with Philippe and his parents would have been the first one.

There is no way I would have pictured myself standing in a glittering hotel room, with four rich Americans and an itinerant monk, staring reverently at a gilded bronze Tibetan Buddha with a sapphire in the middle of its forehead.

Mr Lawrence set the statue on the desk, between

a stack of hotel writing paper and a high-tech lamp. It had the same effect on us all as it had before. Everyone, quite simply, calmed down. Apart from anything else, it was immediately obvious that it was the only thing in the room worth looking at.

I noticed that even Marybeth stopped sneaking glances at herself in the mirrors. Then I felt a bit guilty, remembering that I'd done that, too.

Karel stood quietly by and waited. He didn't attempt to go up to the Buddha. After a pause, he offered to describe specific scratches on it.

The Lawrences gathered round it and tipped it this way and that, looking for each mark as he mentioned it. Every one was where he'd said it would be.

Ruth and I were standing well back from all of this, but I still felt I had to talk quietly. "It only proves he knows it very well," I muttered anxiously in her ear. "It doesn't prove he ever owned it."

"The receipt?" said Ruth.

"As Mrs L pointed out, the receipt could be a dud."

Oddly enough, my main problem was that I wanted to believe Karel. He seemed to me to have the same sort of air of peace about him that the statue generated. What was more, he had it even when he was not in its presence. Also he had told a good story. But was that all it was? Just a good story.

"I have to check up on him," I went on. "I just can't stand by while Mr Lawrence hands over thousands of pounds worth of Tibetan antique."

"It's his money," said Ruth, "his statuette, his business."

"The Basilisk's really worried, though. Look at her!"

"Let them fight it out," said Ruth. "Look – you didn't introduce them to this guy. It's not your responsibility."

"It is, though! I'm in charge of this part of the tour. They're my clients."

"If they'd decided to buy something over-priced," said Ruth reasonably, "or something completely worthless, you wouldn't have felt you had to stop them, would you!"

"I probably wouldn't have known it was over-priced or worthless."

"You don't know now."

"I may not *know*, but I'm suspicious. I'm just not sure. What do you think?"

"I'm not sure either. But if the statue were mine, I think I'd give it to him."

"But it isn't ours, it's theirs. It's very serious, Ruth, being in charge of rich people. They're such an obvious target."

"And they're used to protecting themselves, Jo. They must be or they wouldn't still be rich."

"Look at it this way – what if I do nothing, and they give him the Buddha, and then later they find out they've been had? What then?"

"They probably won't find out."

"If Mr Lawrence tries to go on retreat at a monastery that doesn't exist, they'll find out all right."

"Okay, well then it'll be tough on them. But it won't be your fault."

"Maybe not, but what do you think they'll remember about their European Quest for Antiques Tour?

The nice things they bought and took home? Or the rip-off?"

Ruth didn't answer.

"Exactly," I said. "They'll remember the rip-off. And do you think they'll book themselves onto a Quest Tour next year? Or recommend Quest to their rich friends? It won't matter that it isn't our fault, they'll always associate Quest with something bad happening to them. That's how human psychology works – you ask Gareth."

"Okay," said Ruth. "You've convinced me. So how are you going to check this story?"

I'd rather enjoyed winning the argument with Ruth. It was only now that it was over that I realised what I had landed myself with.

"I haven't the least idea," I said. Then I plodded forward through the huge room until I stood between Karel on the one side, and Lawrences and their Buddha on the other.

"May I make a suggestion?" I said. "I suggest we get this whole story confirmed." I turned to Karel. "If you're genuine," I said, "you won't mind, and if you're not, it doesn't matter."

Karel gave me a smile and a slight bow.

Mrs Lawrence gave me a smile, too, the first real one I'd seen on her face.

Edward nodded solemnly and said, "Good move."

Now, of course, everyone was looking at me, waiting for me to take the suggestion further.

"I'll need the receipt," I said. "And the full name and address of the monastery. And some time."

It sounded good. Only one person in the room

knew me well enough to know I was bluffing, and she wouldn't give me away.

At first Mr Lawrence was quite huffy at my suggestion. But the rest of his family voted instantly in favour of it and then, by way of a clincher, Karel said he, too, thought it was a good idea. "It's best if everyone is easy in their minds," he said.

Either he was genuine or he was calling my bluff. Since I didn't know which, it didn't help much.

Though he was obviously reluctant to let Karel go empty-handed, Mr Lawrence made an appointment for him to return the following morning, at eleven o'clock. The car which would take the Lawrences to the airport to launch them on the next stage of their tour was booked for two o'clock, so that allowed plenty of time.

Karel looked at me apologetically. "The receipt is my only proof," he said, "I find it hard to part with it."

Mrs Lawrence snorted.

"Maybe we could photocopy it," said Ruth. "Leave the original with you."

"That would be kind," said Karel.

Mrs Lawrence announced that my checking was more important than the second half of their Antiques Quest. At first I thought she was letting me off the afternoon tour altogether, but she added, "So we won't expect to set out until four-thirty."

That gave me one hour.

Ruth and Karel and I left the room – where a fresh argument was just starting because Mr Lawrence wanted to keep the Buddha by him rather than return it to the hotel safe – and made our way down to the lobby.

The hotel business centre let us use the photocopier. Karel went away with his precious receipt, leaving me staring at the copy in a bit of a daze.

"Call your mother," said Ruth. "If anyone can hack it, she can."

"I'm eighteen," I said frostily. "I can't call my mother for help the first problem I hit."

"You wouldn't be calling her because she's your mother," said Ruth. "You'd be calling her because she's your boss."

"You don't phone your boss with the first problem, either," I said. "You sort it out yourself."

"Look at it this way," said Ruth, "she's got a phone, she's got a fax, she's got contacts. You could spend an hour on the hotel payphone being passed from department to department in the German Embassy, or wherever, and still not get anywhere. Don't think of her as your boss, think of her as a colleague."

"That's a good idea," I said. "I'll call a colleague."

I called Bill.

Bill works with Mum at Quest Tours – in fact he'd done most of the planning for this one. I think Ruth suspects I fancy him. I don't, not really, even though he is very good-looking and he does have the kind of lopsided smile that some women seem to go for. But he's much too old – he must be more than thirty – and also he fancies himself too much. He doesn't need anyone else to do it.

When I first worked at Quest Tours I was so

beneath his interest that he never looked at me – literally never. As a protest, I avoided speaking to him, but this had no effect because, of course, he didn't notice.

Later, when Ruth and I got back from our Paris Quest, he changed a bit. He even started calling us The Highflyers. Now he does acknowledge that I exist – more or less – and I'd begun to think that he just about regarded me as a colleague, although a junior one, of course. It seemed a good time to put this to the test.

While the phone was ringing, I tried to think how to open the conversation. I didn't want to tell Bill I needed his help, exactly. That sounded as if I was being useless. Mick answered the phone, but he hasn't been at Quest all that long and I wasn't going to trust him with the problem. He put me through to Bill and at the exact moment that Bill said, "Yes?" the right sentence popped into my head.

"Hi, Bill," I said, "this is Jo in Amsterdam. I need a bit of back-up on this one."

And I got it.

To my relief, Bill thought I was right to be concerned. "Fax the receipt through," he said, "and the address of this religious community. I can think of one or two people I can get on to. If they don't know anything, they'll know a man who does. How long have I got?"

"I can give you till ten-forty-five tomorrow, Dutch time," I said grandly. "Karel and Mr Lawrence are meeting at eleven."

"Call me at ten-thirty," said Bill. "And I'll tell you what I've got."

I stopped feeling spaced out and began to feel quite bouncy again.

"Thanks, Ruth," I said, when I'd paid for the fax at reception and we were on our way back to the Lawrences' suite. "Phoning home was the right thing to do."

"You should trust me more," said Ruth. "I'm brighter than I look."

The rest of the afternoon went by surprisingly quickly, despite the fact that we had to take the Basilisk and the Beauty Queen on a trip around the Spiegelkwartier, Amsterdam's antiques-hunting-ground. Mr Lawrence elected to stay behind with his Buddha. Edward said he had another appointment. For some reason I suddenly decided to take Ruth's advice and try being pushy. "Aren't you joining us?" I said. "That's a pity."

"Sorry," said Edward, "I want to go to the zoo. A friend of mine has a temporary job there."

So much for my charm offensive.

"See how successful I am with men?" I whispered to Ruth. "He's not exactly every woman's dream, but I can't even get *his* attention."

"The homely ones are the most difficult," said Ruth knowledgeably. "They're not used to women being attracted to them so they don't react right when it happens."

"I'm not attracted," I said. It was true. "And nor is he." That was true, too.

"You could get him if you wanted him," said Ruth smoothly. "But I guess there's no point wasting effort if he's not your type."

So we left it at that.

I think the two women were still distracted by the
whole Karel thing. They just wandered in and out of
places, picking things up and demanding that things
be taken out of window displays, but not actually
buying anything.

After an hour or so they let it be known they
were ready to be guided back to the hotel, where we
abandoned them with huge relief.

"We'll be with you by ten-thirty tomorrow morning," I said. "And I hope to have some news."

It was only then that we remembered we hadn't
enquired about our luggage recently.

"I'm totally done in," said Ruth. "What do you
bet they say we have to go out to the airport and
collect it?"

They didn't, though, because they hadn't got it yet.

By now a different airline rep was on duty, but she
was as calm as the first one.

"It will turn up," she said.

"When?" I said.

"Soon," she said. "Within a couple of days I should
think."

"I'd throw a crying fit," said Ruth, when I told
her, "but all my tissues are in the case."

We found a café and ordered something to eat.
Then we began to dredge through our shoulder bags
to see if, between us, we had enough toiletries to see
us through.

Before we got very far, though, the food arrived,
and by the time we'd eaten we were almost too tired
to care.

If that sounds weedy, kindly remember that our
flight had been so cruelly early that we'd had to get

up in the middle of the night to be ready for it. And that we hadn't exactly had our feet up ever since.

We made a brave attempt to find a chemist shop, but before we managed it we spotted the tram that would take us to our overnight address. We glanced at each other, nodded, and got onto it.

It was while we were on the tram, staring sleepily out of the window, that I saw something totally unexpected and, somehow, alarming. I thumped Ruth and she looked out just in time to see it, too.

What we both saw, briefly but unmistakeably, were two men sitting outside a café, leaning towards each other across a table, obviously deep in conversation. One of the men was Karel. The other was the man in the blue denim jacket.

CHAPTER TWELVE

Keeping Up Appearances

"I'm really happy I bought that deodorant at the airport," said Ruth. "At least we won't smell."

The tram veered round a corner and clattered to a stop.

"Who cares about deodorant?" I said. "What about that? You saw it, didn't you? Karel and the man in the denim jacket? At a café together? Talking together? I wonder if we ought to go back and ask what they're up to."

The tram whined on its way again, picking up a good speed almost at once.

"Too late now," said Ruth. "And you'll care about deodorant tomorrow, I'm telling you. So will anyone you get close to."

"But what do you think that *meant*?" I said, as the tram reached our stop and we struggled to our feet. "Those two together?"

"I don't know," said Ruth, "but it doesn't look good."

"I think I *will* walk back and challenge them. I'm sure I can remember what street they were on."

"No point," said Ruth. "They'd just make up some good story."

"I suppose so," I said reluctantly. "You're very laid back about this."

"You're not reading the signs right," said Ruth. "This isn't laid back, this is exhausted to the point of death. I've had it for today."

"Fair enough," I said, "I'll leave it till tomorrow. Then I can ask him about it in front of everybody."

"If he shows," said Ruth. "It looks to me as if they know they've blown it. They've decided to give up on the statue and now they're planning their next operation. Shame – I thought he was impressive."

"This is awful," I said. "If Karel doesn't turn up tomorrow, Mr Lawrence will look a fool and I can just imagine how much he'll like that. Maybe I shouldn't have insisted on checking up on him."

"You had to," said Ruth.

"And he didn't mind being checked up on," I said, cheering up. "In fact, he encouraged it."

"What else could he do?" said Ruth. "If he'd argued, we might have got suspicious and called the cops. He's sharp, he thinks fast. My guess is he decided to go along with it and then split. He knows we'll all be moving on soon – he knows he hasn't got to avoid us for long."

"This afternoon you said if the statue was yours you'd give it to him."

"That was before we saw him talking to Blue-Denim."

"But maybe Blue-Denim's a good guy, too?"

"Then why was he lurking and skulking?" said

Ruth. "If he was legit, he'd have walked right up to us in the coffee shop, with Karel."

"I give up," I said. "For now."

We were walking towards our hotel, keeping rather close together. It looked even seedier, now it was dark, than it had in the daytime . . . Even so, we were both so tired that the room looked almost welcoming. Almost.

Then our whole situation came back to me and I let out a sort of moan.

"I couldn't agree more," said Ruth, sinking down onto one of the beds. "I've got nothing to sleep in, nothing to change into tomorrow. I can't bear this."

"It'll be all right," I said, trying to sound positive. I emptied my shoulder bag onto the other bed. "Come on," I said, "tip out yours, too. Let's see what we've got."

Ruth groaned, but she did as I said.

"See!" I said, brightly, "we've each got eye make-up and blusher and lipstick. We've got hairbrushes. We have your new deodorant. We have handcream. This is terrific."

"You forgot to mention half your stuff," said Ruth, picking it over. "Eight peppermints stuck together with fluff, countless tissues, two ballpoints without the lids, numerous packs of airline sugar – and what are these?"

"Bill gives me airline sugar for some reason," I said, "when he comes back from a trip. I keep forgetting to throw it out. And he brought me those, too." I took them from her to demonstrate. "See?" I said. "An airline toothbrush with the toothpaste already on it. Three of them."

"Wonderful," said Ruth. "One each and an extra for whoever swallows hers."

"Why would you swallow it?"

"It's so *small*! I'm not used to scrubbing my teeth individually. Is there any soap?"

"No soap – there'll probably be some in the washroom along the hall."

"And what do we use for towels?" said Ruth.

"He's supplied towels," I said, pointing to the radiator where two of them hung, side by side.

"Good grief!" said Ruth. "You mean those rectangles of grey rag?"

"They're not that bad."

"They sure wouldn't win medals in the hygiene Olympics. Although they look as if they might be able to walk there by themselves. And what about our eyes?"

"Excuse me?"

"We may have eye make-up to put on again tomorrow, but we haven't got anything to take this lot off with tonight!"

"You're not wearing all that much."

"Enough that I'll wake up looking like a panda if I don't do something about it."

"We can use this," I said holding out a tube.

"It's *hand* cream."

"That's all right. There isn't a law that says you can't use it to take off make-up. Any cream'll work." I was beginning to inspire myself. "And we'll hang up our clothes," I said, "so they'll look fine tomorrow. It'll be perfectly all right, no one will ever know."

That was when I thought of it. "Oh no," I said. "No clean underwear!"

"No clean anything," said Ruth, nodding.

"I have to have clean underwear. I can't wear the same tights and knickers for two days!"

"At last," said Ruth, "you're on my planet. I couldn't have stood that girl scout 'don't worry we can clean our teeth with boot polish except we haven't any boot polish' routine much longer."

"I was trying to cheer you up," I said. "You're so gloomy."

"It was you being so cheerful that was making me gloomy," said Ruth. "All that optimism was depressing. I'm okay now. We can hack it. We'll just wash stuff through and hang it on the radiator."

So that was what we did.

It was not the most peaceful hotel to sleep in. Half the other residents came in extremely late that night. The other half came in extremely early the next morning. None of them came in quietly and several of them tried to get into our room. Fortunately, the lock held.

When my watch told me it was time to get up, it was quite a relief. Or it was until I looked at my hair. I'd lain on it badly and the right side of it was sticking out at a stupid angle.

"This is awful," I said, sitting up in bed and staring hopelessly at myself in a blotchy mirror on the wall. "How am I supposed to sort this out without my hair drier or my mousse?"

"Slick it down with handcream," said Ruth. "Like you said last night – any cream'll work."

"It'll make it sticky!"

"That's okay, mousse makes it sticky. Put some on the other side as well and it'll look like you mean it."

It worked better than I thought it would, but it's not a method I'd recommend to anyone who had a choice. I did what I could, then I climbed out of bed to get dressed.

That was when I discovered the radiator had an airlock in it which meant that one half of it had stayed stone cold. No medals for guessing which half of it I had chosen to hang my pants and tights on.

"What's the matter?" said Ruth, seeing me hesitate. Ruth's stuff was totally dry and quite warm. I know this because I was nearest the radiator and I'd handed it to her. She was dressing rapidly and efficiently. "Your things aren't still damp, are they?" she said, stopping in the middle of buttoning her shirt, looking concerned.

"No, they're not damp," I said.

"Good," said Ruth, returning to her buttons.

"They're wet," I said.

Ruth came over to investigate. "You're not exaggerating," she said. "Did you wring them out?"

"Of course I did!"

"Sling them in your bag," said Ruth. "We'll find an underwear shop on the way to the hotel."

"I can't! They'll make everything else wet – and I refuse to go out half-dressed."

Ruth offered to go on her own and buy some stuff, but I said I couldn't bear to be left in that depressing place alone. And what if she got lost?

"I'll just have to put them on," I said. "They're bound to dry eventually."

We'd already decided that, for peace of mind, we'd get to the hotel much earlier than we had to. In fact we'd planned to treat ourselves to breakfast in the coffee shop.

Now, though, I'd realised there was a snag. "Ruth," I said, when we'd paid the aged manager and got ourselves out onto the street again. "I don't think I can have breakfast. I daren't sit down. Damp'll come through my skirt."

"That's cool," said Ruth, "we'll get coffee and a pastry at one of those street-side stalls."

"I can't sit down on a tram, either."

"No problem," said Ruth, "we'll walk. You are walking strangely, though. Are your feet very wet?"

"It isn't my feet that are the problem."

"Ah," said Ruth. "Is it very uncomfortable?"

"Let's just say I know why babies cry when they need changing. You know what – I really don't feel up to facing Marybeth today."

"Little Miss Perfect won't know," said Ruth.

"It's not what *she* knows that matters," I said, "it's what *I* know. *I* know I'm in yesterday's shirt with wet knickers and handcream on my hair. How can I possibly look self-confident?"

"Concentrate on the positive stuff," said Ruth.

"Like what?"

"Like – there's this great-looking coffee stall right across the street – see? Also your skirt isn't creased."

"Wonderful," I said, bitterly, "all I need now is to spill the coffee down my uncreased skirt and my self-image will be destroyed forever."

We got to the hotel just before ten. I hadn't spilt the coffee, but faint damp marks were beginning to appear in the area of my waistband.

I rang Bill from the payphone in the lobby. It was

only nine in London and I was afraid he wouldn't be in yet, but he answered at once.

His opening took me by surprise. "Hey," he said. "Rotten luck about the case."

"How do you know about that?" I said.

"The airline just called – you'd given them this number. They've got it back – the woman who took it didn't realise she had a problem until she started to unpack last night. I've told them to send it straight to Paris. It'll be there before you."

"Great," I said with feeling, "what a relief!"

"I assume," said Bill, "that as a seasoned traveller you had an emergency overnight kit in your hand-baggage?" I could tell he was fishing for details.

"Now you know why I carry such a big bag," I said. An inspired answer, I thought. "What about this Buddha, then?"

"Things are looking good," said Bill. "I faxed the receipt through to the office of the collector who brought the thing back from Tibet. He's away but his secretary verified his signature. So it looks as though the monastery *did* own the Buddha, once. The monastery itself is up in the mountains near the Czech border, and has no telephone, so I haven't been able to find out for sure if it's trying to buy the Buddha back. Or, if it is, if this Karel bloke is genuinely its emissary. Though if he isn't genuine, it's hard to see how he could have got hold of the receipt. I think we can assume he's bona fide."

"Thanks," I said, "that helps. I think."

I considered telling him about the suspicious behaviour of the man in the blue denim jacket, but then I changed my mind. Asking Bill to make enquiries for me was one thing – asking him to make decisions for me was quite different.

"Call again," said Bill, "I've got a couple of feelers out. I may be able to get more on Karel. But I can't see why Mr Lawrence shouldn't give him the statue. His feel-good-factor will soar sky-high – and whatever his family think of his soft-hearted generosity, at least they'll know he's not being ripped off. And – most importantly – they'll know Quest took the trouble to make sure of that. You kids have done a good job."

"Don't we always!"

"You seem to," said Bill, laughing.

"Well," I said to Ruth, when I'd hung up and passed all that on to her, "that's it! Mission nearly complete."

"So why was Karel chatting up the prowler in the denim jacket?" said Ruth.

"We'll probably never know," I said. "But it really does sound as though Karel's a good guy. I'll tell the Lawrences about Denim-Jacket, and I'll tell them what Bill said. No prizes for guessing what Mr Lawrence will decide. Then all we have to do is hang around, being available, until the car comes to take them to Schipol."

"Let's try and work it that we're in their suite at eleven," said Ruth. "I'd like to be there for the emotional moment when Karel walks off with his Buddha."

Bill's praise had reassured me. Also, I was beginning to dry out. "Sure," I said. "No problem."

There was, though. Karel didn't turn up for the appointment.

CHAPTER THIRTEEN

One Tricky Moment Follows Another

There was very nearly a nasty moment in the Lawrences' suite that morning. I'd been so busy fretting about the damp patches on my waistband, and wondering if there were any in worse places, that I'd forgotten about Ruth. I don't mean I'd forgotten she was there, I mean I'd forgotten she wasn't quite as convinced as I was that it was necessary to be polite to clients at all times.

We began well. We knocked on the door at the appointed time. Edward let us in. He was wearing fresh designer casuals, but in spite of that he was looking quite human. I realised I felt quite friendly towards him – and he looked friendly enough himself. Maybe if we got to know each other better . . .

His parents and sister were sitting on a long sofa at the end of the room. If you hadn't known better you could have thought they were posing for a family portrait. In fact, they were just posing.

They, too, were all wearing different outfits today. Mr Lawrence was as expensively casual as his son, but Mrs Lawrence and Marybeth were in formal suits with short tight skirts. Marybeth had a different but equally annoying scarf around her neck.

She looked us up and down and then said, "Oh, I *see*, it's a uniform. That explains why you wear clothes like that, it's because you have to."

The beautiful Buddha was still standing on the desk, smiling his gentle smile, but his benevolent influence didn't seem to extend as far as the Beauty Queen.

Before Ruth had time to say anything startling, though, Mr Lawrence sprang to his feet and swooped forward to greet us. This took Ruth's mind right off Marybeth. As he closed in, she dodged him neatly – but not discreetly. He noticed.

He paused, two feet from us, and frowned at her from under his eyebrows. "Young lady," he said, "I only planned to give you a friendly hug. The kind of hug I would give my daughter."

There was a horribly awkward silence. I felt I ought to break it, but I couldn't think how.

Then Ruth gave him one of her nicest smiles, and said, "Oh, of *course*, I realise that. But I need to keep in practise. Someone like you might not believe this – but a lot of older men actually try it on with people of my age."

She looked him straight in the eye as she spoke, and he looked straight back.

Then he laughed, a slightly strained laugh, I thought, and said, "Well, can you beat it. What can those guys be thinking of?"

"I can't imagine!" said Ruth, and we all relaxed. Especially as Mr Lawrence didn't move any closer.

I began at once to pass on everything that Bill

had told me. Mr Lawrence just shrugged and said, "You've proved my point. Morally, the Buddha belongs back in that monastery."

Mrs Lawrence was clearly impressed, though. "I see you really are taking care of us," she said. She seemed less tense today. I guessed she had decided to accept her husband's decision to give the statue back.

Then I told them about the man in the blue denim jacket – how I was sure he'd been following at a distance when Karel was tracking us back to the hotel, and how I'd seen him hanging around in the lobby when we all came up to the suite the day before, and how Ruth and I had seen the two of them together at a café later in the evening.

Before anyone had time to decide what they thought of that, the telephone rang. Mr Lawrence answered it, said, "Fine, send him up," and replaced the receiver. "He's here," he said to the rest of us. "He's on his way."

I looked at my watch. He was about twenty minutes early, I saw, but that didn't worry me. Or not until Edward opened the door to the visitor.

The man who walked in to the suite was definitely not Karel, with his grey hair and long brown coat. This man was taller, with dark hair, and he was wearing a blue denim jacket.

"Oh," I said, surprised, "it's him!"

The man in the blue denim jacket gave me a startled look, and then turned quickly to face Mr Lawrence. "Good day," he said, in an accent that was entirely different to Karel's. "My name is Julio," (he pronounced it 'Hulio').

"Where's Karel?" said Mr Lawrence. "The desk clerk said Karel was on his way up."

"I am colleague of Karel," said Julio. "I give his name because it easier to explain up here than at desk. I keep his appointment. I here to collect Buddha. You have it ready?"

Faced with Karel, Mr Lawrence had seemed to melt slightly and abandon his banker-image entirely. Faced with Julio, though, he seemed to freeze and become even more bankerly and business-like than he'd been before.

"I have an appointment with Karel at eleven," he said frostily. "You are not Karel and it's only twenty to eleven."

He moved as if to usher Julio straight out again, but Julio caught at his arm – a very bad move, as Ruth observed later – and said, "No, I come instead. Karel say you give to me."

He had glanced at the Buddha, I noticed, but it did not seem to have a relaxing effect on him. In fact he seemed quite nervous.

"I don't like this," I whispered to Ruth. "This one I *definitely* don't trust."

"You're sure it's not just because he doesn't speak such good English?" said Ruth.

"I wouldn't judge someone like that."

"Not even subconsciously?"

"I can't speak for my subconscious."

"Exactly!"

I was relieved to see that Mr Lawrence felt the same way I did. He shook the hand off his arm quite roughly and brushed the sleeve of his jacket. "I don't believe he'd send anyone else," he said. "He'll be here."

"He not come!" said Julio urgently. "He not feel well today. And you go soon. This last chance for monastery."

"He'll be here," said Mr Lawrence again, and he strode to the door, opened it, and waited for Julio to leave.

"Hang on," said Edward. "Shouldn't we be asking some questions here? These two have been seen together, after all."

For a split second Julio looked surprised, I thought. Then he smiled and nodded. "Exactly," he said. "We good friends. We from same monastery."

"So where is Karel – why can't he be here?" said Edward.

"He sick," said Julio. "He not strong man."

Mrs Lawrence rose to her feet and took a few steps across the room. "You're a long way from your monastery," she said, in a sympathetic voice.

"A long way," agreed Julio, relaxing a little.

"Whereabouts in India is it?" said Mrs Lawrence smoothly.

"No," said Julio, frowning. "Not India. In German mountains."

"Neat one, Mrs L," said Ruth to me quietly.

"I've been judging people all my working life," said Mr Lawrence, unmoved by Julio's correct answer to the trick question. "And I've never been wrong."

I realised this was a speech he made often.

He glared at Julio. "I'd like you to leave," he said.

"What I tell Karel?" said Julio. He seemed close

to tears. "I tell him he cannot have promised Buddha because he sick?"

"Hey, Dad," said Marybeth, unexpectedly. "You did say you'd give it him!"

"I said I would give it to Karel," said Mr Lawrence, every inch the Banker now. "I expect him here shortly."

He opened the door and stood by it. It was absolutely obvious that Julio had two choices – walk out or be thrown out. He walked. Mr Lawrence shut the door firmly behind him.

Edward moved over to us. "This is all a bit weird," he said.

"Too right," said Ruth.

"I have a suggestion," said Edward. "I think we should follow Julio."

"What'll that do?" said Ruth.

"I've no idea," said Edward. "But I'm going to try it anyway. Are you with me?"

"We're with you," I said, without hesitating. I already knew we worked well as a team. "But we'd better move fast. I just heard the lift go."

CHAPTER FOURTEEN

Tracking and Trailing

The three of us raced down the stairs rather than wait for one of the other lifts.

"If he's left the hotel by the time we get to the lobby," Edward panted, "we'd better split up and go in different directions."

"So how do we contact each other if one of us finds him," puffed Ruth. "You got a portable phone?"

"Not on me," said Edward. "If we get separated, we rendezvous in the hotel coffee shop."

"Slow down," I said, as we reached the ground floor. "Don't attract his attention."

There didn't seem to be any danger of that, though. Julio was just crossing the huge reception area, towards the automatic doors onto the street. His hands were in his pockets, his shoulders were hunched, he looked thoroughly fed up. He walked in a straight line through the crowded lobby, not looking right or left, and certainly not looking behind him. It seemed he had no idea that anyone might follow him.

In fact, we tracked him easily down seven streets and around seven turnings without any trouble at all.

We simply walked along about ten yards behind him. Then each time he disappeared round a corner we ran up to it and peered round it. There he would be, plodding ever onwards, and we would give him a few seconds start and then go on again.

"What are we going to do when we find out where he goes?" I said.

"Depends where it is," said Edward.

"Do you suppose he's going back to Karel?"

"Could be."

"This is crazy," said Ruth. "This is no way to follow someone! In a group! Talking!"

"It's working, though," I said. "He has no idea, and we haven't lost him yet." I was enjoying myself.

"Anyway," said Ruth, as we reached the third corner, "what's with all this stealthy stuff? We think Karel's a good guy, right? We know he and Julio are buddies. So why don't we go right up to Julio and ask him to take us to Karel?"

"Because we're suspicious of Julio," I said.

"That's prejudice," said Ruth. "It's because he's South American and doesn't talk English so good."

"It has nothing to do with his nationality," I said crossly, "it's his shifty eyes."

"Hey, Edward," said Ruth, "why didn't your father ask Julio for Karel's address?"

"When Pop gets an idea fixed, there's no shifting him," said Edward. "You heard him – he still thinks Karel's going to turn up and he doesn't rate Julio. He wouldn't expect to get a truthful answer, so he wouldn't bother asking."

"Will he mind that we've all chased off after him?" I said, suddenly anxious. It had happened so fast that

I'd let myself get caught up in it. Really, though, I ought to be back at the hotel, in case the Lawrences needed me for anything.

"He'd have yelled at us to stop if he'd thought it was a bad idea," said Edward.

"I saw his expression as we left," said Ruth. "He looked cool. The Basilisk looked pretty horrified, though."

She and I both realised what she'd said the moment the words were out of her mouth. We kept very quiet, hoping Edward hadn't heard. It was a feeble hope.

"My mom can look a bit fierce," said Edward, grinning, "but I don't think she turns people to stone."

"I'm really sorry," said Ruth. "It just slipped out. I forgot you were one of them. For a moment there, I was thinking you were one of us."

"Thank you," said Edward. "What's my nickname then?"

"We call your father the Banker," I said hastily, remembering the one nickname that wasn't in any way offensive.

"And me?"

"We call your sister the Beauty Queen," said Ruth rapidly.

"I thought you might have a worse name for her," said Edward. "She's given you a hard time. She's not that bad, really. I think you'd like her if you got to know her."

"Sure," said Ruth.

"No, really. Mom nagged her into going in for those competitions and now she feels she has something to live up to."

"That can't be too hard," said Ruth.

"She *is* very pretty," I said.

We were both as keen as each other to keep Edward's mind on Marybeth.

"The problem is," said Edward, "that she's intimidated by you two."

"Never!" I said.

"It's true," said Edward. "Don't forget, I do know her quite well. Here you both are, travelling around on your own, doing a great job at hunting down pickpockets and checking up on unexpected monks, and there she is, trailing around with her parents, like a little kid. She's decided to put you down before you get a chance to put her down."

"But we weren't going to put her down!" said Ruth.

"She didn't know that."

We dodged round the sixth corner. There was Julio, stomping on at a steady speed. We gave him his space, then herded round the corner together and followed.

"You're obviously not going to tell me what you call me," said Edward wistfully. "It must be truly awful."

"Oh, hey, it isn't *that* bad," said Ruth. "As a family you're known as the Banker, the Basilisk, the Beauty Queen and the Other One."

I thought fast and added, "It's a compliment in a way. We could tell you were different." Then I wondered if I'd thought too fast. In trying not to insult Edward, it seemed I had insulted his entire family.

"It's okay," said Edward. "I know I'm nothing to look at."

"You have a really nice personality," I said, surprising myself. "You don't act rich at all."

Edward grinned again. I would like to tell you that the grin transformed his whole face and turned him into a dreamboat. I'd like to tell you that, but I can't, because it didn't. But it was a very nice grin. "Don't worry," he said. "Animals like me, and that's all that matters."

"Humans are animals, too," said Ruth, so softly that only I heard. She was feeding me a line. She meant me to try it on Edward. But I couldn't.

Then the inevitable happened. We watched Julio disappear round the seventh corner. We hurried up to it. We peered carefully round it. And Julio was nowhere to be seen. This time he had disappeared completely.

"I knew it couldn't be that easy to tail someone!" said Ruth.

We were in a long canalside street. There were houseboats moored all along one side and small shops, bars and cafés all along the other. He could have turned into any one of them. Or, if he had suspected he was being followed and had decided to run for it, he could probably have got as far as the nearest bridge on the one side or the nearest side street on the other.

We stood still for a second, in silence.

Then Edward said, "Okay, now we *do* have to split up. I can run – I'll go on ahead and work my way back. You two check all these places." Then he took off at speed.

"That seems to be what he's best at," said Ruth, gazing after him, "running across bridges after people."

"I don't think Julio can have got that far," I said. "I'm sure he didn't know there was anyone behind him."

"We'd better do what Mr Masterful said," Ruth went on, "and check out all these joints."

"I'll do that," I said. "You stand here, somewhere discreet, and watch in case he comes out of one of the houseboats."

"You got it," said Ruth.

I worked my way along the line of shops and cafés. I sidled casually into each one in turn, glanced round surreptitiously, and then sneaked out again. As I went, I thought how interesting it was that even someone quiet, like Edward, couldn't help thinking he was in charge, just because he was male.

Each time I came back out into the street, without having found Julio, I caught sight of Ruth's brilliant hair, glinting in the sun near a canalside tree. She obviously thought she was being unobtrusive, but if Julio was in one of the houseboats he would be almost certain to spot her.

I didn't really believe he was in a houseboat, though, I believed he'd gone. I thought it was very likely that we'd never see him – or Karel – again, which would make an extremely unsatisfactory ending to this particular bit of the Quest tour.

The last café I went into seemed very dark after the sunlight outside. I went right up to the bar, as if I was going to order something, and then turned and looked at all the tables. If anyone offered to serve me, I planned to say I was looking for a friend, but that the friend didn't seem to have arrived yet.

The friend – if that was the word for him – had arrived, though. He was sitting at a table in the far corner with two women, one quite old, the other middle-aged. He had his back to me but I recognised him at once. The middle-aged woman was leaning across the table saying something to him. The old woman was mopping at her eyes with a handkerchief.

As I watched, Julio stood up, shrugged his shoulders, and walked out. I hurried to the doorway.

Julio was walking off briskly towards the nearest bridge.

Edward was in the act of crossing back over it.

Even though he was some distance away, with his back to me – I saw Julio see Edward. I also saw Edward see Julio. Half a second later I saw Julio take to his heels and run. A millisecond after that, Edward was running after him.

They disappeared round a corner.

I looked in the other direction. Ruth, who had obviously seen what had happened, was running towards me from her treeside hideout.

"That looks bad," she gasped, as she reached me. "He took off the second he saw Edward. That has to mean a guilty conscience."

I glanced back into the café, at the two women at the corner table. Then I caught Ruth's sleeve and towed her over to their table with me. I was aware they might not speak English, or that if they did they would probably tell me to mind my own business, but it seemed worth a try.

"Excuse me," I said, "I'm awfully sorry to bother

you, but I have reason to believe the man you were just talking to may not be very honest. May I ask if you know him well?"

Ruth said later it was the most pompous speech she'd heard me make in her life. It worked though.

The women, who turned out to be German tourists, fell over themselves to tell us the tale.

The day before, the older one had bought an antique brooch from a jeweller's shop nearby. When she was not far from the shop, Julio had stopped her and explained that the brooch had once belonged to his sister, who was desperately ill. It had been stolen from her a year ago, he said, and he had been searching for it ever since. He had been happy to find it in the shop – but had not had enough money to buy it back.

"Sounds familiar," muttered Ruth.

His sister was now dying, Julio had told her, and he begged her to allow him to borrow it for a few days, to make his sister happy in her last hours. When she was finally laid to rest, he would return the brooch.

The old woman had almost believed him, but had told him that her daughter would be very angry if she made such a rash decision on her own. So she'd made a date with Julio, at this hour, at this café, and had brought her daughter along too.

"That must be why Julio called at the hotel early," said Ruth. "He wanted to get back here on time."

The daughter told us she had not believed the tale for one moment – especially as Julio had refused to allow the two women to take the brooch to the dying girl themselves. Realising his plan had failed, Julio had stormed out.

"And then you came in," said the daughter.

The old woman, who had been crying over the fate of Julio's imaginary sister, cheered up at once when she heard our story, but her daughter was furious.

"We shall go to the police instantly," she said, rising to her feet. "Do you think your friend will have caught him?"

"I hope so," I said. "But I don't know. I'll give you some numbers where you can contact us if you need to, but as soon as we can, we'll go to the police ourselves." I scribbled down the name of the hotel and Quest's London number. "One way or another, I think Julio's going to end up in gaol."

"Why," said Ruth, watching as the two women hurried out of the café, "aren't we going to the police station right now, with them?"

"Because we have an urgent appointment," I said. "We now know what Julio is – what do you suppose that makes Karel? And while we're here and Edward's pounding all over Amsterdam, Karel is probably conning Mr Lawrence out of a rare and hugely valuable Buddha."

"Good grief" said Ruth. "How fast can you run?"

CHAPTER FIFTEEN

Citizen's Arrest

I don't know why I was surprised. The whole reason we were rushing back to the hotel was because we thought Karel might be going to turn up. Yet when I saw him in the enormous lobby it somehow gave me a shock.

Especially as he looked so peculiar.

Ruth and I had run most of the way back. We'd wanted a taxi, but didn't dare waste time waiting for one to cruise by. So we'd set off on foot, hoping to pick one up as we went. We failed totally, and by the time we tottered through the automatic doors, we were windblown and out of breath.

"There he is," said Ruth pointing.

And there he was. He was holding on to the stem of a tall, ornamental indoor tree, halfway between us and the lifts. He was swaying slightly on his feet and staring fixedly down at the ground.

"Hell fire, he's drunk!" said Ruth. "Why don't they throw him out?"

"It's so crowded in here, I don't suppose anyone's noticed him yet," I said.

I realised, with relief, that this meant we could slow down a bit.

Karel was not in the Lawrences' suite, poised to make off with the Buddha, he was swaying harmlessly about in the foyer.

I remembered Edward had suggested the coffee shop as a meeting place if we got separated. I decided we had time to check it out quickly to see if he'd made it back. I'd just got as far as the doorway through from the foyer, when I saw Edward coming in by the street door. He weaved his way towards us, dodging the tables, looking as wild-eyed and flushed as we did.

"That Julio sure can run!" he said, as he reached us.

I remembered how fast Edward had rushed across the bridge after the pickpocket the day before. It seemed impossible that Julio could have outrun him. Then I realised that, of course, Julio would have had all sorts of advantages. He knew the area and Edward didn't. He would have known which turnings to dodge down, which alleys had two exits, that kind of thing.

"It doesn't matter," I said, reassuringly, interrupting Edward before he had time to explain, or apologise, or whatever he was trying to do. "We're in time to warn your parents. Let's go straight up."

"Karel's lurching around near the lift," said Ruth, pointing, "smashed out of his skull."

Edward looked, frowned, and then went straight over to Karel. As we watched, he took him by the arm and began to talk to him. Ruth and I looked at each other, shrugged, and walked over to join them.

As we got there, Edward was leading Karel to a chair against the wall and holding his arm as he sank down into it. Then he crouched in front of him and said, "Do you know what he used?"

Karel reached into the pocket of his long, brown coat and brought out a glass phial. "Yes," he said. "He left it beside me." He handed it to Edward.

Edward looked at it and whistled through his teeth. "This is heavy duty stuff," he said.

"Stupid of me," said Karel. "I did not understand what he was going to do until the needle was in my arm. It did not all go into me – there was still some left in the syringe."

"He drugged you?" I said horrified.

"Who drugged you?" said Ruth at the same time.

"Julio," said Karel calmly. He smiled at Edward. "I feel better for the moment," he said. "It comes upon me in waves."

Edward, meanwhile, was feeling Karel's pulse and tipping his head to the light to look into his eyes. "Even if you only had half a dose," he said, "I'd have expected you to be unconscious for two or three hours at least."

"Is he going to be all right?" I said.

"Yes. I can't believe how well he's dealing with it," said Edward.

"It is my training," said Karel. "It is the yoga. I cannot neutralise the chemicals in my body, but I can control my reactions somewhat."

"Are you in good general health?" said Edward.

"Very," said Karel.

"You sure? No medical problems at all?"

"No problems," said Karel. "Are you a doctor?"

"No," said Edward, "I'm about to qualify as a vet."

"Excellent," said Karel contentedly.

"He's more drugged than he seems," said Ruth.

"Not at all," said Karel. "I have always had more trust in vets than in doctors. A man who can treat a frog or a turtle or a giraffe or a chimpanzee must be more competent than one who restricts himself to the higher apes."

"Even so," said Edward, "I'm going to call the hotel doc to have a look at you." He turned to us, "I'll go talk to them at Reception," he said. "Why don't you two take Karel up to the suite. The police'll be there by now."

He hurried off, leaving me bleating after him, "The police?" and feeling that I was losing my grip on the situation completely.

Karel stood up carefully, ready to come with us. He didn't seem in the least worried at the thought of the law.

Ruth gave me a friendly pat on the shoulder. "Don't look like that," she said. "You can't always be in charge of everything."

There are times when a friend can understand you much too well. That was one of them.

"You like to be in control yourself," I said frostily.

"Only of my own life," said Ruth, "not of everyone else's as well. Chill out! You've done great!"

The next half hour was frantic.

Karel gave us a brief version of his story as we went up in the lift, but he saved the details until we were in the Lawrences' private sitting room.

The sitting room was not a peaceful place.

There were two policemen standing by the window

– a senior one and a junior one. There was Mr Lawrence, standing protectively over the Buddha. There was Mrs Lawrence, pacing about, looking sharp-eyed and alert. Finally, there was Marybeth, sitting on the sofa looking bored and trying out different styles with her neck-scarf. They were all talking at once.

As soon as Ruth and I got there, we joined in. We couldn't really help it. We had important information they needed to know. Karel was the only one who remained quiet. I explained what had happened to him and showed him to a chair. Then the senior policeman called a halt to all the chatter and said that he thought we should all hear what Karel had to say.

Karel, his voice only slightly slurred, was quite willing. The junior policeman took out his notebook and prepared to write.

"Julio is a professional man," said Karel. "He spends time near those places which sell antique treasures. He watches until he sees a customer who looks – what shall I say? – 'innocent'. Then if this innocent customer purchases something small enough to carry and precious enough to be worth the risk, he approaches with a heart-rending story. It will soon become apparent to the innocent purchaser that there is only one way to ensure that the story has a happy ending, and that is to hand over the small and precious object. Later, Julio will sell the object to connections of his, and it will disappear out of the country and never be seen again."

"I seem to have heard this story before," said Mrs Lawrence sharply.

"Precisely," said Karel.

The senior policeman was nodding. "We have known of him for some time," he said, "but we have not had sufficient proof."

Then we all stopped and looked round as Edward came into the room. With him was a woman carrying a small black bag in one hand and the phial Karel had given to Edward in the other. She went directly to Karel and began to take his pulse. Karel continued talking as though nothing was happening.

"Julio had been following me for some time," he said. "At first he assumed I was a rival. It was an easy mistake to make. There I was, searching around the galleries, yet I do not look as though I am in a position to buy expensive works of art. When I located the Buddha and told my tale – my true tale – to the gallery owner, Julio was there, listening. I noticed him as I left the gallery, but I had no idea then that he was spying on me."

The doctor rolled up Karel's sleeve, stared at a small mark on his arm, and then proceeded to take his blood pressure.

A sudden ringing sound from the desk at the side of the room made us all jump. For one second it seemed to be coming from the Buddha itself. In fact, of course, it was the telephone. Mr Lawrence picked it up. We waited. "Right," he said. "Okay. Got it. You want to talk to her or are you going to tell me?"

I guessed it was Bill, and began to move towards the desk. Mr Lawrence kept the telephone to his ear, though, listening and nodding and grunting questions down it. I stopped moving. Clearly Bill didn't want to talk to me.

When Mr Lawrence had finished with him, he

handed the receiver to the most senior-looking of the two policemen, who began to do his own listening and nodding and grunting of questions.

Clearly Bill was willing to talk to anyone except me.

"Julio saw that I didn't persuade the gallery to permit me to take the Buddha," Karel went on.

The junior policeman took up his pen again.

"But unlike the gallery owner, he believed me. And he saw, as he thought, a chance to add an innocent monk to his plan and double his profits. While I kept vigil near the gallery, to see if anyone would buy the Buddha, Julio kept vigil too, watching me. When he saw me follow you, he knew you must have the Buddha. He followed, too, with no particular plan, to see if there was some way he could take his opportunity."

"Why *did* you follow us?" said Edward suddenly. "That's what I've never understood. Why didn't you come right up to us at once?"

"I could not speak with you in the gallery," said Karel, "because the owner had not believed me and would not have permitted it. And if I had approached you in the street, you would have brushed me off and hurried away, would you not?"

"I guess so," said Edward.

"I knew my only chance of persuading you to listen to me would be if I came to you formally, on your own territory – somewhere where you felt secure and not threatened."

The senior policeman put down the phone. I caught Mr Lawrence's eye and said, "Was that my office?"

"It was," said Mr Lawrence. He raised his voice and spoke to the room in general. "Karel's in the clear," he said. "The monastery confirms his story." He looked at his wife. "A lot of time and motion could have been saved if you'd trusted my instincts," he said. "I told you, I never make a mistake. But let that pass."

"But we saw you and Julio together," said Ruth to Karel.

"Did you?" said Karel. "He followed me away from this hotel and then caught up with me and persuaded me to go to a café with him. I didn't see you there?"

"We were passing in a tram," I said.

"Ah. Well, that was when Julio offered to act as an agent for me. He said he had much experience of tourists and that while an unworldly monk might fail to convince them, a man of the world such as himself would be sure to succeed. He said that if I would give him the money I had, he was certain he would be able to acquire the Buddha for me. He thought he had seen his chance to have the money *and* the statue." He laughed. "It is a common mistake," he said, "to assume that a man who is not interested in worldly things must also be stupid. It was then that I guessed how he made his living, and when I challenged him with it I was certain – by the way in which he denied it – that I was right. I do not need to tell you that I declined to co-operate."

"Very wise," said Mr Lawrence. "I never trusted him for a second."

"Not entirely wise," said Karel. "I did not guess that he already knew my lodgings, or that he would come there today to put me out of action. I should have thought of that. I was not paying sufficient attention – and I have suffered for that. However, it enabled me to hear his full story. He held me down until the drug began to take effect – and could not resist boasting of his successes."

When he had finished, there was a short silence. Then the doctor remarked that he was surprisingly well, but said she would like to keep an eye on him for a while.

And the senior policeman said he would appreciate it if we would all go down to the police station and make formal statements. The two German women were there already, he said. "This time," he added, "we do have enough evidence."

"It's a shame you didn't catch Julio," I said to Edward.

Edward looked at me with such a strange expression on his face that I wished I hadn't said anything.

"Don't feel bad," said Ruth, who had also seen his face. "You tried."

"But I did catch him," said Edward, aggrieved.

"Indeed he did," said the senior policeman. "Julio is in custody."

"These guys drove me back here," said Edward. "They came straight up to the suite, and I came in through the coffee shop to look for you."

"Brilliant!" I said, and without thinking I gave Edward a friendly pat on the back. He responded by giving me a hug, just with one arm, which was surprisingly pleasant. Then almost at once he turned and looked at Ruth. He was obviously hoping for some praise from her. Ruth smiled at him and said, "Great!" but she didn't move towards him. Edward looked vaguely disappointed. I had been right – I didn't even appeal to the Other One.

"Now what?" said Mrs Lawrence testily. "We have a plane to catch."

I switched my brain back into guide-mode. I don't want to boast, but I did do well! As Ruth says, being responsible for rich people does something to me. I persuaded the police that as they had the German tourists, Karel, Ruth and me, they didn't need the Lawrences as well. They had to give contact addresses, of course, but they were able to leave in their airport limo as planned.

Before they went, Mr Lawrence had time to get on to the gallery where he had bought the Buddha and arrange for them to collect it from the hotel safe and have it shipped direct to the monastery. He also remembered to give them the necessary details for a fresh export permit.

Mrs Lawrence had time to thank us for what we had done.

Edward had time to give Ruth his address in case she felt like getting in touch when she went to New York to see her father.

Marybeth had time for one final insult. "Edward's always picking up strays," she said quietly but audibly.

"Somehow," said Ruth to me, also quietly but audibly, "I don't think I would get to like her if I knew her better."

Right at the very end, after we'd seen the Lawrences into their car, Mr L lowered his window and called out to me, "Sorry, I forgot, there was a message for you from that guy Bill in the London office. He said to tell you that you've had a postcard from Rome." He gave me a huge wink. "From a guy called Tom. Says he's having a good time."

"Thank you," I said, and the car pulled away. Something most peculiar began to happen inside my rib cage. I think I may have been having palpitations. Edward might prefer Ruth, but even I had to admit it really was beginning to look as if Tom fancied me.

"Hey!" said Ruth. "So are you still so sure he won't call when he hits London again?"

"I can't think about that now," I said, feeling a bit flustered. The junior policeman was holding the car door open so that we could get in next to Karel. "We haven't finished this yet."

"That's cool," said Ruth, getting in after me. "This is our second visit to a Dutch police station in two days. We can handle it." She gave me a hefty nudge. "We can handle anything – we're the Highflyers!"

I grinned back at her. "Yes," I said. "Yes, I suppose we are."